ENEMY DADDY BEAR

MOSSY RIDGE SHIFTERS 1

SAMANTHA LEAL

PAMELA AVERY

CONTENTS

CHAPTER 1

"Well, shit," Monica whispered to herself as she pulled into the driveway. Her chestnut waves fell into her face as she looked at her house. She absolutely loved this place. Her brother, Frank, was sitting on the porch with a sheepish expression. He always looked that way. He was the best. Her brother gave her faith that there were good men out there, after all was said and done.

"Hey, Frank, whatcha doing here?" she said aloud, with a smile.

He gave her a sly smile, "Brought the kids a pack of smokes and a beer, Monnie, what else am I good for?"

Monica snorted. "Get outta here, Frank. You're not allowed in any liquor store for fifty miles." He snorted back, the same snort; because it was one of the many things they had in common. He was her safest and best friend. She sat down beside him on the steps, leaned over, and rested her head on his shoulder. Their matching chestnut hair, side-by-side, made it look like an ad for autumn. "Man, today was long, Frank. Is there anything up or are you just here to cheer me up?"

Frank reached around her shoulders and gave her a squeeze. "Well, I've got a problem with a bank loan. I think I have it figured out, but it isn't for today. Today, I'm just here to say hey… and I fed the kids some supper from the freezer. Hope you don't mind. I'm sorry if that was overstepping."

The voices of two kids overlapped each other as they yelled from the house, "It was disgusting, Mom! Pizza! From the *freezer*" one voice said.

"I'm never talking to Uncle Frank *again*! He made me use a *napkin*!!" said the other.

The comments were followed by barks and laughs of the pre-teen sort, fading as the boys moved away from the windows. Frank laughed and called into the house, smiling, "You punks better be cleaning up in there, or I'll block you from the Hut!" Groans and snorts came in reply.

Monica stared at him and choked back a sob. "*Oh my God,* Frank, I was dreading even thinking about dinner. Thank you *so* much! It's the most thoughtful and concretely helpful thing you could possibly have done. You just gave me a whole night. A whole night!" It was astonishing how fast her emotions flew when she was home. Who was she kidding? They flew everywhere, all the time lately!! Her deep green eyes were full of tears already, damn it. She couldn't believe how close her emotions were to the edge today!

She always thought she had it so together, and someone does *one* nice thing and all her work in keeping up the façade of 'having it all together' just exploded into pieces. She did her best to push her fears away, just about every day. She looked at him in tears, smiling slightly, "And don't think I won't find out more about the bank loan. It will just have to wait 'til I'm done with my breakdown…" Frank smiled down at her.

Sigh. There were some days it was just all too fucking much.

Ugh, she chastised her inner sailor for all the swearing. It was a joke with Frank and the kids, and all of her oldest and best friends. Nobody would ever guess what a foul mouth she had. She could completely hide it. It never showed at the office, the PTO, the Town Council, ever. Not even when the situation completely called for it. If you could stick a microphone in someone's mind, hers would be the most profane ever heard. A lot of times, it made her laugh; it felt more authentic somehow. It had taken a lot of therapy to get to this point, but she accepted it. Her pint-sized body contained a six-foot salty-mouthed sailor, and she couldn't seem to fix it. She rolled her eyes at herself and looked over at her brother.

Monica blinked hard several times, to try and clear her mind of the criticisms of the past. She grinned at Frank. She had no idea how he ran an entertainment center for kids. But he did, and he did it well. The Bouncy Hut was a raging success, according to everyone, but only she knew how much he had overcome to make it a success. She was so proud of him.

In many ways, The Bouncy Hut felt like the center of town, at least for her. Her kids spent all their spare time there, and Frank was actually a quiet father figure to a lot of the kids in town. He'd managed to learn a different way, somehow, from how they'd been raised. It was nothing short of miraculous. The way he loved her boys blew her heart wide open.

It had been a long day, but look, she had an entire evening free of chores and hustle. It was a miracle! She and the kids could just tuck in and watch a movie or maybe she'd even drag out the board games she kept buying in hopes they'd eventually do a 'game night'. *Oh my god, that was it.*

"Frank, come on in. I think we're doing game night. We'd love a fourth...whaddaya say? It'll only take a few hours off your life...I think today's game might be Monopoly. You know you're the best at the money. Wink, wink." she said in a wheedling voice. She backed into the door of the house, waving him in.

Frank laughed, "Oh God, this is going to be horrible..."

reat, Billy's naked. It was time to get into the car and Billy was running, full speed, around the kitchen island, yelling and windmilling his arms. He was a 'helicowter'. But he was determined to make the best of it. Tim put Billy's clothes down on the island and stepped in front of the whirlwind child. He leaned down quickly and grabbed Billy's chubby torso and lifted him off the ground. "…. And blastoff!!!!" he said. Tim flew Billy through the air, around the island, to his delighted squeals. In a few minutes, Tim sat himself down and trapped Billy with his legs to get him dressed. Underwear first, then shirt, then pants. Socks and shoes had to wait for the car; it was the only solution Tim could see. At least then Billy would be manageable, strapped to a chair in a smaller space.

Tim smiled and scooped Billy up again, carrying him over his brawny shoulder like a sack of potatoes. The irony of how he, supposedly a "big bad bear shifter", was, in many ways, outmatched by a child was not lost on him. "Time to go, Captain Bill. This time, your driver does the work. You'll have to tell me how to get there, though, navigator." Tim got him plugged into the car seat and his socks and shoes on. Billy was burbling and singing the song of his favorite cartoon. Tim watched him in the rearview mirror and felt his heart expand a little more. Yes, it had been a bit of a battle, as it kind of always was… *Like herding cats*, he mused, but nonetheless, he had to admit, it was an amazing thing to be a parent, and these were the little moments that would get him through it.

He sighed.Billy *was* the best thing around. He also appreciated that, more and more, it was only in moments like this that he felt any semblance of what he imagined humans might consider "peace". He was used to his Bear raging and always being just beneath the surface, yearning to break free.

Tim was a shifter. The rush of finally letting that animal side of himself take over was akin to what he imagined every adrenaline junkie in the world was after. But it was beyond that… It was also somehow becoming more of who he was lately…in every way. That part was fine; he was used to having the Bear inside of him, but the part that was driving him crazy? More and more, it seemed, his Bear had an incessant yearning for a mate. It had been 4 years now since the woman he thought was his forever mate had left. That was a pain he preferred not to dwell on. If it were up to him alone, he would have been done with mates, at least that's what he told himself. For a while, he had been able to keep his Bear at bay in that department. The occasional conquest had kept things in check. He never let his heart get involved. That was on permanent lockdown.

But his Bear didn't really seem to give a shit what he wanted. More regularly now, he felt restless…anxious. The Bear was feeling irrational and almost dangerous, like a ticking bomb. He had heard stories of what happened to those who fought their Bears. It wasn't pretty. But he wasn't about to give in any time soon. Just a few more years. Then, maybe, he would be ready to think about a mate… maybe…

He knew he should talk to his brothers about the feelings, but he couldn't even imagine how to put it into words.

* * *

TIM SQUEEZED HIS HULKING FRAME THROUGH THE DOORWAY and into the trailer a little sheepishly, if that was possible for a man of his size. He was late again, and he hated that. It wasn't that he'd get in trouble – he worked with family – but it just didn't match who he was. He was a man of integrity and honor, and showing up on time was a given, a sign of respect to everyone. His son, Billy, was four, but still in the terrible twos, it seemed. It was unreal how complicated it was just to get out of the house. The 'helicowter' routine was a relatively new wrinkle…and it was kicking his ass. It had taken twice as long to get dressed, a million hours to get any food in him, and he'd been a devil to get into the car seat. *He wasn't built to put children in car seats; he was meant to run and fight and – and mate…*He pushed his Bear's compulsions from his mind. Despite the relative bliss of the parenting moment afterward, with everything on his plate, he was tired. It was just 9 a.m., and he wanted nothing more than to just have a beer, or 2, or 6, and call it a day. Hopefully, that would get his Bear to simmer down. It used to do the trick at least.

He looked up from the doorway to see a smiling Alice looking at him. "Oh boy, Tim, looks like little Billy was a handful today." Alice was his brother's new wife and the manager of all things at their company, Ursa Development. She had twins of her own to deal with; although now, she had Bill to help out. Bill was the oldest of the brothers, and it was great to finally see him so happy, and instantly, a family man. As far as Tim could see, they were quite an ideal little family, on the same team; pulling together to keep it going.

He wished he could say the same for himself. He'd had that, or so he thought, at least for a little while. Then, a year after little Billy came along, off she went. Just like that. Terri had left a note saying she was done with the whole 'little mama' thing. It had been hard to even comprehend, let alone handle. She was his mate. He lived for her. He lived to see her safe and cared for. Every moment, he was aware of her; he would have fought any adversary, crushed all comers. He would have done *anything* for her. He was left stunned, his Bear inconsolable – wounded to the core. It was as if he hadn't even existed to her. Just like that, the bond had been severed. She was just done with the work of caring for the baby and was gone.

For a while, it had been all he could do not to either drink himself into a stupor or crush anyone who was stupid enough to let him goad them into a fight. In fact, in the beginning, he had purposefully made trips to some distant towns just for the purpose of stomping some belligerent ass. His brothers and the other packs knew enough to give him a wide berth. He still had days when his heart was sore, but they were getting fewer and farther between. While he and Terri had been together, his life was all about her. But now, with time, he could see that his loyalties had clearly been misplaced. Perhaps some deep wound had allowed him to feel their bond had been real. When she just up and left, and he realized it had never even been close to those things. His Bear had Wanted, so badly, to claim, to protect, that he had been blinded. *Never again*, he told himself.

Raising a toddler and trying to work full time was enough to keep him distracted most of the time. He tried not to think about women too much, and Billy was young enough that he'd have no memories of ever having a mother like Terri. Tim knew that was a sour apple, though, since his own mom had left when he was a little older than Billy. Knowing that some women just don't love their family enough leaves more than a bad taste behind. Tim and his brothers all had their issues because of it. He'd be watching Billy like a hawk as he grew, to give him whatever he needed, to make up for the loss. His brothers – Bill, Mike, and Curt – all had their own mom issues to work through. He wanted Billy to have a better start. It would make his life as a shifter easier as he grew up.

He couldn't give little Billy all the brothers he'd had, but he'd sure give him the solid dad he needed. His Bear hummed in satisfaction. The connection to the primal force was something Tim knew as the most central power in his life, and he was looking forward to helping Billy discover it, when he came of age. He and his brothers had provided each other the support they needed or tried to.

For the Lawson boys, being so close in age meant that they'd done their first shifting very close together and adding that to the drama of regular human puberty, made for some trying times. There were times when the household of boys was empty, all four of them having 'run away' or 'gone Bear' to escape the confines of the house. No woman in the house meant a level of wildness that they all still felt, to different extremes.

Tim's failure in his marriage to Terri was something he associated with 'not knowing about women', because his mom had taken off so early. The fact that Terri was a shifter should have made it easier but didn't. Terri seemed to be the opposite of him; she wanted the shifter power to be all that she was, and she ran wild, as if the shifter in her was more animal than woman. It was just beginning to dawn on him, years later, that it might have been about Terri and not about him at all. They always say time heals all wounds, but it was actually true for him, and for his brothers. They were all making their way forward now. Even with all that behind him, Tim still couldn't help a spark of jealousy when he saw Bill and Alice together. Imagine that, a partner, a woman who *can* handle it all. There were days it was all just too much for him. Sometimes, just seeing Alice brought it all back.

Alice looked at him more closely, "You okay, Tim? Having a rough time this week?"

Alice always seemed to know. Maybe it was that good mother instinct.

Tim shook the memories off. "I'm okay, Alice. I'm just feeling worn thin today, I think. Maybe I just need a stronger coffee." Tim smiled ruefully.

"Well, we've got really crappy coffee brewing in the back. But what I think you really need is a good minute or two over at Harriet's. Go get us some good coffee? Get yourself one of those fancy ones you like and breathe for a little. This work here will hold; there is nothing that needs doing first thing. Harriet and Max will be glad to see you."

Tim didn't even resist. He started backing right out the door. God, but he needed the break – a kid-free, happy, adult break.

"Don't forget to bring me back my Americano!" Alice called.

CHAPTER 3

*H*arriet and Max were bustling behind the counter. The place was always quietly humming as people from all over liked to sit and read, chat, pull out laptops and do their work in a vibrant but peaceful place. It helped that the coffee was always delicious and strong. They'd named it The Cup when they came into town a while back, and the brother/sister team was still arguing over whether it was half-full or overflowing. It surely didn't matter to Tim; he just needed a quiet spot to soak in his caffeine.

Harriet greeted him with a smile and a wave. Max tipped his head, which was as much as one ever got from Max, really. Max was a Wolf shifter. He was a quiet one, a real loner. He'd left his pack several years ago and stuck close by his sister to keep from going completely feral. Shifter Wolves were like that; they needed family nearby or there was a good chance they'd just surrender the human to the animal. Bears were a little more solitary, but Mossy Ridge was pretty packed with Bear shifters these days, and Max was very welcome, as long as it was all under control. The Lawsons made up the Bear pack. With Bill as the Alpha, they ran the show in Mossy Ridge, at least, behind the scenes.

There had been a little excitement last spring when another Wolf had shown up. The Wolf had been tracking Max and ended up stalking Alice – Bill's Alice. The Wolf had been seeking Max to apologize and bring him home but had been willing to kill him if he said no. Max said no.

The shifters in town dispatched him quietly to the regional Shifter Tribunal, with Max's help. It was a court, of sorts, but also a seat of power. They served all shifters. They had a way of getting information from shifters that was beyond the Mossy Ridge pack's ability. It was critical not to let word of Max's location get back to the original pack. Rumor had it they were significantly bad news. It had been a serious and sad event, and Max's role in the town had become more central. If a Wolf could be part of a Bear pack, Max was one of them.

Tim stepped up to the counter and placed his order. His Bear was acting a little funny, he wanted to get some coffee in his system. The Bear had been rumbling since he opened the door to The Cup. There was something going on in here, something he'd have to keep his eye out for, but he could not imagine The Cup containing any threat. He wondered, with each step he took, what it was, but let it subside as he thought about the coffee.

He'd pick up Alice's Americano on the way out. He just wanted to sit down with the town newspaper and have ten minutes of quiet in his day. He moved to the next counter to wait for his coffee to be made and bumped into a beautiful, perky bosom wearing a lime green sweater. He looked down at the tiny body next to him. The bosom was so perfect that all he could think of was licking the cream off a key lime pie, right through to the nipples he could imagine there. His cock thickened immediately. *Well, there she is. She's what I've been looking for,* Tim realized with a slight shock. His Bear was trying to push through, roaring, *in a coffee shop.* His Bear had never reacted that way to a woman before, not even Terri.

"Fine, Tim, just fine. You go first, no, really, go ahead." Tim realized the bosom was speaking to him. The sarcasm dripped from the voice of the green sweater so heavily that it caused Tim to wince. He looked up and saw the vaguely familiar face of a woman squinting at him. He could swear he heard her inner world calling him a 'fucking bastard', but nothing came out of her mouth.

He looked down again and saw that he'd caused her to spill her fresh hot coffee all over the front of her green sweater, without even being aware. "Oh my god! I'm so sorry, ma'am, let me help." He went to grab paper napkins and present them to her lime green chest, just barely halting before rubbing a stranger's breasts in public. They were really pretty, nice breasts, but still. His Bear really wanted to touch them. He looked up.

If looks could kill, Tim knew he was a dead man.

The woman backed up slowly, blinking furiously, looking very, very angry. She took a deep and grabbed the napkins from his hand. "Ma'am!? Thanks, Tim, but I'm not 78. I'm your age! In a real hurry to get more coffee, Tim? Didn't little Terri make you enough this morning?"

Now, it was Tim's turn to step back. He squinted his eyes at her. *Did he know this viper? Why did she look familiar?*

"I'm sorry, miss. I really didn't mean to spill your coffee. Do we know each other?"

"I'm Monica Smithson, well, Jones to you. We went to school together, Tim Lawson, and we've been at the same Council meetings lately. Thanks for remembering." She smiled with pleasure at the embarrassment flushing Tim's cheeks.

She started to unpeel the green sweater from herself,

exposing a silky black camisole over her pleasingly round breasts. She dabbed at her cleavage with the napkin. Tim was definitely watching and trying not to get caught in the act. The way they were being jostled was exactly how he would do it himself. His Bear was settling in to watch. Tim could feel his cock twitching more. His Bear was definitely up to something. *Oh, good lord, Tim, what are you doing? Viper, Remember?*

"At least the coffee won't show up on the black, so I can still go to work. If I had to go home right now, I'd probably think about a lawsuit."

At that, Tim's head snapped up to her eyes. The growing lust evaporated. "Look, Monica. I do remember you now, mostly from the Council, frankly. I'm sorry about the coffee, and I'm sorry I don't remember you from school. I don't remember a lot from that time, and truthfully, I can't imagine why I'd *want* to remember a *sweetheart* like you. Take care now." With that, Tim turned and left the shop. As soon as the door closed behind him, he remembered Alice's Americano. He threw his hands in the air.

* * *

MONICA FUMED AND FELT LIKE CRAP PRETTY INSTANTLY. HER temper was ridiculous. *Oh my god, that guy's eyes! How was she still breathing? He was the most gorgeous man ever, always had been!* Why had she jumped on him like that? A lawsuit? Really? It had definitely bothered her that he didn't know who she was. Why did it hurt that he didn't remember her? She'd certainly always remembered him. Those Lawson boys were always in trouble, but Tim had been the nice, smart one in the mix. His shoulders alone made him pretty memorable. Agh. This was not how a grown woman behaved.

Her ex had always hated her outbursts and had ridiculed

her in private anytime she spoke out with her temper. Her luck with men had been all bad, all the time. He had lied to her as much as her crappy dad and was the source of some mighty fine inner turmoil, still, after all this time. Between her dad and her ex, Monica was not a big fan of relying on men. At least divorce was a real thing; it's too bad kids couldn't divorce their terrible parents.

She needed to take some more deep breaths. Tim had bumped into her, that's all. His shoulders deserved more than threats. *What? His shoulders were broad and strong, but what did that have to do with anything? Oh my god, she was so turned on.* She got most of the coffee cleaned up and got a new coffee to take with her. She heard Max take an order for an Americano over the phone and then he said, "Sure, Tim, no problem, I'll bring it out."

Monica raised her hand. "Max, I'll do it. I owe him an apology for jumping on him like that."

Max raised his eyebrows at her, "You sure, Monica? I don't want this going any further. This is a peaceful place, just like our parents had always wanted for us. Keep it calm."

Monica sighed. "Yes, Max, I'll keep it peaceful like the hippies, I swear."

He handed her the coffee with a slight smile and she loaded up to step outside. Between her bag, her sweater, and the two coffees, she was well and truly hands full. She backed out the door of the coffee shop and turned slowly to get her giant purse out the door. She rolled her shoulders and turned to look for Tim.

It didn't take long. He was cozied up on the bench with the most ridiculous woman she'd ever seen. Her hair was brassy red, the box kind. Her boobs were bursting from the top of her tank like kids reaching for candy. The makeup on her face alone would cover the full bodies of several young children. If she didn't know Mossy Ridge was clear of hookers, she'd swear Tim had just picked up a hooker, in Mossy Ridge! Tim looked so clean cut next to her. His jaw was set firmly, and his sandy hair caught the late summer sun. *Those freaking eyes. Like sun on water. Oh god. He's so beautiful, I want to lick him,* Monica thought. *What?!* The tramp, however, had her hands on Tim's strong arms and was looking directly into his face. Monica's skin flushed with totally irrational anger. Her town. Tim was *her* friend, even if they hadn't talked for, well, ever. This was *her* town, and people like this did not belong here. People like that should *not* have their hands on Tim Lawson's arms. She barely recognized the discomfort on his face before she loudly said, "Tim! Tim Lawson! I have your coffee and need to talk to you right now. *Now.*"

Even through her rage at the floozy, she recognized she was being way too loud. She was *way* too jealous. She felt like her face was on fire. What the hell was going on with her? He was married! He didn't even remember her! Where was her unflappable cool?

At her words, both heads had snapped to look at her. Tim's look of relief *did* actually penetrate her emotional overload this time, and she wondered if she'd inadvertently saved him in some way. The floozy just arched her eyebrows and sat back slowly from Tim, resting her hand on his thigh in a clearly possessive manner. Tim gently moved her hand and stood to approach Monica.

"Which one?" he said, leaning toward her. *Oh my god, he smells so good. How can he smell that good?!* Monica was flustered by his closeness and took a minute to raise the Americano toward him.

Tim looked closely at her and whispered. "Did you really need to talk to me or were you just rescuing me?" His large hand brushed hers, wrapping around the Americano and a couple of her fingers and her skin was instantly hot where they connected. The world seemed to thud in line with her heartbeat. Monica could feel his warm breath on her cheek, and immediately felt her whole body respond. It had been a long time since a man had been so close to her. She was mortified to realize her nipples were hardening as she looked up at him. She could feel goosebumps on her skin. She closed her eyes. She took a deep breath of his scent. He was so damn *manly*. Her breathing was getting faster. This was out of control. She *had to get herself under control!*

"Why would you need to be rescued, Tim? Big strong man like you? Don't want your wife to know you're into the floozy type?" Monica heard the viciousness from her own mouth in a completely surreal way. Usually, when she was this quick to slay, it had something to do with her ex. This one was completely unprovoked. She put her hand on his arm to fix it and felt the sting as she realized it was too late to take it back. Tim was already backing away.

"Uh, sorry, Monica, this is Kaylie, my *ex*-wife's little sister. You must not remember her from school; she was much younger than we were. Kaylie, Monica. Enjoy each other. Kaylie was here visiting a friend. Thanks for the coffee, Monica." Tim continued backing away, winked and raised the coffee to her before turning and walking away.

Kaylie got up and sauntered over to Monica. She leaned in and whispered, "Nice rack, sister." Monica's eyebrows went through the roof, and Kaylie laughed and gestured to her chest, where all her cleavage was showing over the top of her black lace bra that was completely exposed, the camisole having slipped completely down when she was overloaded and coming through the door. Kaylie strutted off, laughing, and Monica dropped everything but the coffee to cover up her chest.

"Oh my God, oh my God," Monica muttered, her entire body flushed with embarrassment.

CHAPTER 4

Tim made his way back to the office, alternating between annoyance and curiosity. Tim *had* gotten a pleasant eyeful of breast that morning, and he had smelled her faint arousal. His Bear was all set to make a move. But the boobs didn't outweigh the venom he'd heard coming out of her mouth, right up to including Terri. Geez. What the hell was wrong with that woman? What'd she have against him? He would've loved those breasts against his chest; it had been quite a while since he'd been so interested in any. The green eyes were lit up with sparks like he'd never seen before. There were tiny fireworks in there. Her hair had smelled so good, and that camisole? He hadn't seen so much of a woman for a long time. He was damn curious about her. The peek he got at her cleavage was replaying in his mind, over and over.

What the hell made him want her so bad? His Bear was on fire with desire. He could have lots of women in town, or so his brothers kept telling him. He wanted to pick that mad, venomous little woman up, throw her over his shoulder and bring her home to bed. She was just so damn cute. His Bear loved the way she smelled, and Tim couldn't get those eyes out of his head. He was taken aback by the strength of his Bear's desire. Maybe someone had hurt her in the past and that's why she lashed out. Maybe she just needed to be taken care of the right way, like in a steady Bear kind of way.

He brought the coffee in to Alice and asked what she knew about someone named Monica. Alice had her finger on the pulse of the whole town somehow, and he knew she'd know. "Monica Smithson? Tell me you didn't start a fight, Tim, just tell me."

"What? Why would you even ask that?" Tim said. "She was practically spitting at me for bumping into her, and she was throwing Terri's name around like we were still married. I don't even know why she already hates me."

"Oh brother, Tim, you've got to start paying attention. She's on the Town Council, remember? She single-handedly shot down the playground proposal last year, *single-handedly*, and all for her brother's bouncy house place. She was convinced the playground was going to impact her brother's business. It was a completely obvious power play, as far as I heard. You were actually there."

"Crap. *That* lady? I didn't even recognize her!" Monica's cleavage popped into Tim's mind immediately. Maybe he hadn't been completely looking at her face the whole time. But he did remember the Council meeting that she chaired, and the utter disdain she'd shown for the Ursa Development proposal for the town playground. His brother, Bill, had been on point at that meeting, Tim was just standing support. He remembered how tired he'd been; little Billy had been sick all that week. It seemed ages ago. The decision had been so clearly biased – so clearly an issue of old townies protecting their own – it had really soured the brothers, again, against the town. This was a town they protected, they loved, and they were still fighting the same prejudices, now, that they'd fought in school.

"I hope you didn't ruffle any feathers, Tim. We're going to need her approval again, on the development of the Mathewson property." Alice quirked an eyebrow at him. "Did you? Did you ruffle her feathers? Just tell me now and I'll start damage control. She's quick to attack but just as quick to forgive and move on. My kids know her kids and I might be able to smooth things over… just tell me."

Two of Tim's brothers – Mike and Curt – came in just then, stopping short when they saw Alice's upraised eyebrow. "What did Tim do?" piped up Curt in a singsong voice. Curt was the youngest and was always on the lookout for someone else to finally be the one in trouble.

"Shh, Curt, let's listen and find out what Tim has to say for himself," said Mike. Mike was the muscle head of the group, with a fantastic lumberjack beard and tattoos all over, but his looks were very, very deceiving. His brain was as big as his bicep, or much bigger. But you'd have to see the biceps to judge. They were like small watermelons. Mike raised his eyebrows and looked curiously at his brother.

Tim put his head in his hands. "Oh my God, Alice. I definitely put her in her place, I think. Or she put me in mine, I don't even know anymore. I think feathers are ruffled, pretty damn much, yeah."

CHAPTER 5

$\mathcal{A}$lice didn't waste any time. Before Tim could escape for the day, she'd hooked up a playdate for all the kids – hers, Monica's, and Tim's – and arranged for Tim to be the babysitter so she and Monica could go out for drinks. "I figure you need to do some of your own suck-up legwork, Tim, and taking care of her kids will definitely gain you some ground toward forgiveness. God knows I need a night out. And Billy will love being surrounded by the big kids. He'll sleep like a log when you get him home, I promise."

Tim's eyes were wide. "You want me watching five kids? Tonight!? And one of them is my own terrible toddler? Alice! I'm not prepared for this! They'll kill me, I'll be completely killed!"

Alice laughed right in his face. "Tim, Daddy, get over it. You're a big, strong, hunk of a man, you can do this. In fact, you'll find it a breeze. Just tell the big kids to watch the little one and serve them all pizza. It'll be over before you know what happened. My kids don't get to see other kids that much, except at school, and you know they love Billy. Relax,

Pops. It's on, and it's in a half hour, so hop to it. My house in thirty, dude. Go get Billy; I'll meet you there with the pizza."

Tim turned tail and called over his shoulder, "Billy likes cheese."

Alice laughed and raised her eyebrows, "Ha. Like I've never done this before?"

TIM AND BILLY PULLED INTO ALICE'S PLACE WITH ITS BIG OLD porch, and found Alice's kids, Leah and Ryan, sitting together on the porch. *"Billy!"* they yelled, and Billy started squealing in his car seat. Tim laughed, pulled him out, and let him go. The kids and Billy ran off around the back of the house.

Alice called to Tim from inside the house, "You might not see them again before the pizza arrives, Tim. Mine were talking about showing Billy all around the rocks in the back. They've named it, *The Glen*. Bill said you guys had named it something similar when you were kids."

Tim shook his head. They'd called it *Faehill*. It was interesting to be back here so many years later, with his own kid. Uh, plus some extra kids. He shook his head again. He just couldn't believe that more kids would be easier than just one.

He turned as Monica's sleek black car pulled into the drive. Two boys spilled out of the back, tearing past him and around the house to join the other kids in their glee. He heard a quiet *"Crap"* as the front door of the car opened. Eyebrows raised, he turned more fully to see Monica slide out of the car. His Bear growled in appreciation. She was wearing a t-shirt and jeans, both as tight as could be, but managing to look classy and comfortable all at once. The t-shirt hugged her curves in a way that caused a definite twinge in Tim's pants. Her hair was down in chestnut waves around her shoulders. She looked so perfect, a perfect little bite of a woman. Tim noticed all of her curves, again, but wasn't distracted by any venom or lime green this time. He caught himself looking for signs of her nipples through the tee shirt. He wanted to flick those things so badly…maybe just with his thumb… but his tongue would be pretty damn good too. He started moving towards her, he could feel the animal in himself, stalking.

"Get enough of a look, Tim?" Monica croaked, her venom caught up somehow in her throat.

Tim pulled back, his lust interrupted, *Ah, there it was,* thought Tim. *Time to charm.*

"Sorry, Monica. You can't blame me, can you? You look wonderful. Men must look at you all the time." Tim was a little surprised at the not-so-faint feeling of jealousy he felt at the thought that it was probably true.

Monica actually blushed, cleared her throat, and took a deep breath. "Ehem, Shh, Tim, I am busy feeling awkward and mad. You are the only man who looks at me like that, believe me. Don't confuse me, I'm mad and embarrassed and awkward and geez, my god, I just have to stop talking!"

Oh my god, thought Tim, *she's adorable when she's confused. What?! The viper is adorable? What is going on?* Tim's Bear was on all fours now, watching Monica, nearly panting with desire.

Tim took a deep breath. He had to get his beast under control.

"Okay, okay, I'll dial it back a little for you. I'm here to watch your kids, Monnie. Can I call you that? Alice assures me that more is actually merrier, and that I will survive. I'm hoping this makes up for spilling your coffee this morning. I really didn't mean to." Tim put on his best puppy dog eyes.

Monica laughed nervously. "That's dialing it back? Holy

smokes, man. Those eyes. Sheesh. Watching the kids for the night, for free, is worth more than my spilled coffee, by about a million. I was in a rotten mood this morning, so I'm sorry too. I really am, I didn't mean to jump on you about Kylie, and I didn't know about Terri, but I shouldn't have been so vicious, either way. She was really awful to me in school. I've not been sleeping well lately and… and I can't guarantee you'll survive tonight. It's like, 50-50, I think. My boys are on fire today. But I'm sure Alice and I will be back pretty soon, really. I haven't been out for drinks for about three years, so…and yes, Monnie is fine, my brother calls me that." Monica stopped, as if realizing she'd just been blathering, again. She blushed and blinked furiously, trying to get herself back to cool, calm and collected.

Tim was enthralled. His Bear was standing up, roaring his approval. Tim stepped again toward Monica without thinking, his cock taking the lead.

Alice called through the window, "It's going to take at least three hours, you two. Nobody is in any hurry, and I'll be damned if *I'm* going to hurry. Tim, Bill is on patrol tonight and will stop by to say hey. Uh, Monica, he's, uh, joined the Safety group that started up in this neighborhood, did I tell you? I'm almost ready, hold on…"

Tim stopped. He found himself standing very close to Monica. He looked down at her. His Bear was growling and really, really turned on. *What had he been thinking? What was he going to do, grab Monica and run away with her?*

Alice appeared at the door, cash in hand. "Here, Tim, pizza should be here in the next hour. Leah knows how to work the remotes, and make sure they all wash up when they come in. If we're not back, have them in pajamas by 9 at the latest, but they can crash on sofas till we get back, okay? You've got our cells, I think… Monica, did you text him yours?"

Monica pulled out her phone and looked up at Tim as he recited his number. She was looking at him like he was a morsel to be snacked on. He watched her lick her lips as her eyes traveled down his body. He was a thousand percent sure she had no idea how transparent her attraction was.

Tim felt his phone vibrate in his pocket. It distracted him a little from the pulse he was feeling from his cock, but only just a little.

"It'll be fine, Tim. Text me if the boys are trouble. They're named Luke and Brian. Luke is older, but a mischief-maker. Trust Brian, he's got the darker hair. I guess I'm letting Alice plan out the night, see you later!" Monica looked over at Alice and the two women almost scampered over to Alice's beat-up Subaru. They were already laughing as they got into the car.

Tim couldn't help feeling a little jealous; it would feel really good to be going out with Monica tonight. It had been a long time since he'd been out with friends, or a woman with an ass like that. Tim shook his head. His Bear side growled lightly as he watched the car pull out.

He turned with a sigh to face the house and the inevitable chaos within.

CHAPTER 6

*A*ll in all, it was a great night, unbelievably. The kids were completely self-sufficient, they spent most of their time outside, and when it was time to eat and watch a movie, the older kids swept little Billy along like a tumbleweed. There was no drama at all; it was a night full of laughs. Tim already knew Alice's kids, but Luke and Brian were a trip. Luke was, as warned, a total mischief-maker and Brian was a serious but jovial ten-year-old. They were interested in animals, science, and action. Tim couldn't believe it, but he legitimately enjoyed himself.

Bill had stopped by after they'd had their pizza. The Bears were patrolling the woods behind the house. There'd been another rumor of a Wolf this week, and they were leaving nothing to chance. Tim didn't think there was any danger after the last Wolf so thoroughly, disappeared, but he was glad to see Bill in the middle of it all. They'd talked and discussed the patrol schedules for the week ahead. Bill took off into the woods again after a few minutes. Tim could just barely make out his shift at the edge of the woods. There was always a little shimmer to the air when a shift occurred.

After that, the movie began.

He'd actually fallen asleep during the movie, with boy children all around him. Leah had set herself up in her own chair as the queen of the living room, but the rest of them all managed to be touching him somehow. And he loved it. He felt completely at home, no matter that he'd been completely bamboozled into doing it. He wondered if he could get Alice and Monica to let him do it again, or maybe Monica could stay and snuggle too. His mind was pretty one-track about Monica, it seemed. Looked like he needed to get his Bear some air, or at least a good run, to shift back to responsible father from lustful beast.

Alice walked in on the scene, late in the night, the TV flashing blue on the kids. Everyone was in pajamas, and everyone was asleep, in what probably resembled a Bear den in winter. She stepped over pillows and blankets to wake Tim. "Hey, Papa Bear, I need you to take Monica and the boys home, her car won't start. Wait. Why don't you just leave the boys here? Let me check with her..." Tim untangled the limbs and pulled Billy up onto his shoulder, still fast asleep. He was out like a rock. He made his way to the door and saw Alice coming up from Monica's side, while Monica was kicking the tires of her car and swearing a blue streak. It was quiet and under her breath, but Tim and the Bear heard it loud and clear.

Alice rested her hand on his arm, "It's okay, Tim, she's just mad about the car. It's a real nice-looking piece of crap, just like her ex."

Tim walked slowly down to Monica, making as much noise with his feet as he could without waking Billy. He knew enough not to surprise a wild animal. Monica turned as he approached, cheeks flushed, and saw the sleeping Billy and immediately calmed. She grabbed her purse from where she'd thrown it, checked that everything was in it, and started walking alongside Tim's truck.

"What's up with the car?" Tim whispered as he slumped Billy into his car seat and buckled him up. Monica was climbing into the front seat and let out a harrumph sound.

Tim got into his seat and looked over at her. She was awful pretty, Tim thought. It was nice to have a woman in his passenger seat, made him feel more whole somehow. She was brushing her chestnut hair back from her face and tying it up as women do. He got a nice long look at her curves as she did, her breasts rising and falling gently, and felt his body stirring in response.

"That car is like most of this town, and all of my life, Tim, a big fake. Pretty on the outside and a piece of shit on the inside." Monica was flushed, Tim realized. There was more than one reason he was driving her home, he saw. Still, he was intrigued by her looser way right now, and it made him laugh on the inside to hear her swear. It seemed to suit her, in a weird way.

"Have a good time with Alice?" Tim raised his eyebrows at her.

Monica laughed quietly, "Oh my god, it was good, Tim. I don't get away from the kids and the work and the every-thing enough, you know? I almost forget I'm just Monica sometimes… I love that Alice girl, I've known her since forever, you know, even if we move in different arenas now."

"What is your arena, Monica? I haven't seen you much beyond the Council."

Monica looked down as Tim started the truck. "I don't know, Tim. It's the Council and the Design Group, the kids, my brother, that's all. No friends; just work and family and fucking strong boundaries. I keep everything fucking together, for all of them."

"What do you get for you, Monica? What's just for you?" Tim was surprising himself with his questions. He was taking advantage of her willingness, he guessed. He didn't talk to many women outside of Alice, and it was nice to have someone so willing to talk.

Monica looked a little lost right then. She turned in the truck and faced him fully. "I've got nothing, Tim, except my family. And as much as I love and am devoted to my brother, it's not like it's even. He needs a lot from me, and I give it, all the time. Because what else is there? I'm not even sure I like my work anymore. I work with too many pretentious fuckers, and I'm exhausted by all the work I have to do to maintain the goddamn illusion that I care about them. I'm fucking exhausted by all of this shit." Monica's eyes were welling up with tears. "I just want to go to some inn somewhere, with a king-sized bed, have a lot of sex and sleep, and be fed hot pizza with cold beer. That's all I want in this life, Tim. What the fuck is wrong with you?"

Tim's eyes were watering; he was trying so hard not to laugh at her idea of paradise. He was snorting and trying to smother it and half bent over the steering wheel. He wiped his eyes and looked up at her with a giant smile.

Her face relaxed and she leaned back against the door. "What are you laughing at, dork? I'm telling you my fucking dreams like a goddamned idiot, and you are laughing?"

Tim whispered, "You're basically describing the truest desire of every straight man in the world, Monica. Every.Single.Man. Me included. I would *die* to give you lots of sex, pizza, and beer. I'd even let you sleep occasionally."

Monica's eyes went round. Tim's gut squeezed again, and he laughed silently as he snorted and clutched his gut. Monica started giggling. "Men. I have missed men. You can be so much damn fun." Monica looked in the back seat. "I can't believe Billy hasn't woken up with this snorting going on. Are you going to take me home or what, Tim Lawson?" She was smiling softly, leaning back on the window.

For a second, Tim thought she meant something different and then he remembered he was driving her home, to her house. He was mildly surprised to feel disappointment about that.

"Monica, I haven't laughed like that in a long time. It would be my pleasure to drive you home. Where the Hell do you live?"

* * *

As they pulled into her driveway, Monica was still smiling, and Billy was still miraculously asleep.

"Thanks for the ride, Tim," Monica turned to say, but Tim was already out of the truck and coming around to her door. "What the frig!? He's opening the door for me? What am I, in a romance novel?" she whispered aloud.

Tim opened her door and put out his hand. "What the heck, Tim? You think I can't get out of a truck by myself?" She started to get turned around.

Tim put out both hands to stop her, "Monica, I am trying to cop a feel." He smiled. "That better? That suit you more? If my chivalry makes you uncomfortable?"

"Ha!" Monica laughed. "Taking advantage of a drunken lady? Now that's something I'm familiar with!" Monica leaned out into Tim's arms, he grabbed her around her hips, and she slid down his front till her feet touched the ground. It was a long, slow slide, and her breasts slid down his chest, his hands running over her ass. Her head came to a stop in the middle of his chest. The tension in the air was immediate and crackled with the heat. Tim was immediately hard.

Monica stepped back to stand against the side of the truck and Tim moved in to stay pressed to her. He put his knee between her legs and brought his face down to hers. Tim leaned in to smell her neck.

Monica grabbed his face and looked up at him. "Could you please kiss me, Tim?" His Bear growled deeply. He put his hands on the truck behind her, body pressed tight to hers and went in low for the kiss he'd been wanting for the past hour. He started with a soft-lipped kiss as he felt her body lean into his. His cock stirred with her body so close to his, and he felt her respond. He could smell the faint scent of arousal from her, and it made his eyes roll back. He wanted her so much that it was hard to control himself. He wanted her right then and there, by the side of the truck. Monica's eyes were closed. Tim's tongue darted out to her lips, testing, and Monica's response was immediate, hot and fast. She leaned into the kiss, probing deeper with her tongue, toying with his, sucking on his lips. If a kiss could be actual sex, this one was. Tim's brain had shifted into looking for places to lay her down so he could get her naked and watch her writhe beneath him. He wanted to taste her pussy. He wanted to put his fingers and his cock in that beautiful woman. He wanted all of it....

"Pa?" Billy murmured sleepily from the back of the truck.

"Fuck," both Monica and Tim whispered at the same time. Tim pulled back and looked at Monica. It was like waking up from an intense dream. He wasn't sure what was real and what was dream. She looked up at him and smiled, a little shakily. She put her hand on his chest and lightly pushed.

"Okay. My God. Well, good night, Tim Lawson." Monica was breathing heavily. "I've got to go have a very hot shower for the next hour. Or maybe cold. You go get your boy back in bed. Okay?" Monica took a deep breath and steadied herself on the side of the truck. "I'll see you around, Tim. Thanks for watching the boys, and thanks for the ride home." She grabbed her purse from the truck and did a slightly weaving walk up to her door while Tim stood, still holding her door.

"Hey, Monnie?" he called quietly. She turned. "I'm going to see you tomorrow, you know. Put money on it." Tim closed the truck door and walked around to the driver's side. He pulled out, watching Monica shake her head and head into her house, lights flicking on as she went.

"Woah," Tim said to himself.

* * *

THE NEXT MORNING, TIM HAD BILLY UP EARLY, TO GET AN early start on making it to daycare and work on time. Billy was quiet and got ready in record time, and Tim was actually early to work, walking into a quiet trailer at the work site. He started making coffee and sat in the office space he'd painted just last season. It was a really beautiful little space Alice had made. Women really had the touch to make places homey. He wondered what Monica's place looked like inside. He shook his head. He hadn't been drunk last night; he'd been stone cold sober. What had made him so clear in his own feelings? He'd told her to look for him today. Was he even going to do anything about that? He had to. Did she even remember it? She was still a little buzzed when he dropped her off. Would she know if he didn't follow through? Didn't he want to see her again?

She had certainly made an impression on him last night. He'd had sex dreams for the first time in a long, long time. Monica's green eyes flashed at him in the dreams and her chestnut hair along his chest was a high note, as far as he could recall. He'd woken with a swollen cock and had needed to take a cold shower just to start the day. He couldn't believe he was acting like such a schoolboy. All he wanted to do was throw her down and have his way, making her scream his name in pleasure. His Bear was sharpening his claws in anticipation of seeing her again. What was that about?

CHAPTER 7

Monica was pleased that she barely had any headache in the morning. The house was quiet as the kids were still with Alice, and she'd had two or three big glasses of water before turning in last night. She lingered in bed, her thoughts drifting back to Tim, wondering if it was just the alcohol that had made last night so fun, so full of potential. She was no spring daisy, she wasn't dewy-eyed for him, but a nice guy to tussle with in bed would not be turned down, and maybe he could be that fun guy that in no way got in the way of her life. She bet she wouldn't see him though; it was just one of those moments in a truck that fizzed like a soda pop.

It wasn't going to amount to anything. He'd probably hide out for a couple of days and she'd see him at the Council's next meeting, as if nothing had happened. And truth? Nothing really enormous did happen, it was just a kiss. It was just that potential that simmered there, just possibility. She tended to misread men anyhow, it was her fatal flaw. She never knew what the truth was behind the man. The men she'd known the best, her dad and her ex, had been truly excellent liars. It was pretty hard to trust anymore.

It was nice to have a moment's quiet after all that. The summer was ending, and the kids would be back in school soon, but a morning like this, with no breakfast to make? Amazing what it could do for her. She could feel her body waking up, her breasts perking up, along with her thoughts. Those shoulders, man. Tim did that for her, she thought. Just a little bit of male attention, and her body lit up. Even now, again, she could feel her pussy getting wet, just remembering Tim standing by the truck, his hot body pressing against hers, top to bottom. *Oh my god, that man. She'd been pretty ready to let him have his way and had some ideas of her own. His fucking shoulders. The eyes! Oh man, she'd never even seen his ass! Oooooooh, man. It was crazy how sexy he was.*

It had been really, really hot, and she hadn't felt so turned on in a long time. She would've been fine with a quickie right up against the truck, in the driveway and all. That thought kind of blew her mind. She hadn't been aware that her need was so close to the surface or that she even had those needs. Damn, it didn't even bear thinking about, how long it had been.

Monica let her fingers drift down her belly to her pussy. She had gotten wet just remembering that kiss and the bulge in Tim's pants. She wondered what kind of cock Tim had, and if he knew what to do with it. She had a feeling he did and thinking that made her nipples peak with hardness. Monica sighed, and smiled. It had just been a kiss, really, and she was happily amazed by how much it was reverberating. She could still feel him pressed up against her. It made her feel sexy and wanted, and it was a flipping great feeling.

Monica lounged some more and rolled herself out of bed and into the hot shower. Ten minutes later, she was dressed and on her way to pick up the boys before heading to work.

She had had to borrow her neighbor's car to get to work as little Miss Crocker wasn't driving anymore. Her car was in the shop until they figured out what was wrong with it this time. The boys were spending the day at their uncle's place, a full day of no screens. She wasn't sure they could handle it, but it was on Frank, thankfully. Frank was a saint, especially considering how they'd been raised.

Frank had always received the brunt of their dad's physical abuse. All dear old dad had done to *her* was lie, lie, and lie. But Frank had gotten massive doses of adult scorn and belittling, along with a few well-placed rib shots. Being a tough broad was all she could do to keep from still being afraid. She still had fears that Frank would fall apart, that he'd fail, and it would be her fault this time. She'd been so afraid as a kid, there was no one she could trust to be the rock, and it made everything feel precarious, all the time. But she trusted Frank, and that was enough. Frank smiled at her and chuckled at her quick mention of her late night as she dropped off the boys.

She left them shrieking happily and pulled slowly into the design office parking lot. She noticed a truck in the lot but didn't think twice about it, really. It reminded her of Tim briefly and she couldn't stop a smile as she climbed out of her beat-up, borrowed, golden Cadillac. It was not a shy piece of automobile, that's for sure. Miss Crocker had inherited it from her brother, and evidently, it was quite a source of pride.

As she smiled her way to the office, she heard, "Do you always smile on your way into the office? Is it the swanky car? Or did something really nice happen to you lately?" His voice was so damn sexy. She turned to see Tim climbing down from his truck. She couldn't help but smile brighter. His jeans hugged him in all the right places. He had a simple tee that framed his biceps and just about forced her to imagine putting her hands on them. She could bet he smelled of soap and warm skin. Her pussy immediately tightened, and her breath caught. He had actually come for her; damn it, he was so damn hot.

She was overwhelmed with the flood of sensations she felt at seeing him. He had come, just to see her! She was a giddy school kid again. She wanted to actually spin around in joy! The adult woman in her couldn't decide if she wanted to run away or start taking off her clothes. She had no idea how to react, was she supposed to be cool right now?! What did she expect this man to do, throw her down on the pavement and ravish her? She was so mad and scared and so embarrassed by herself, all at the same time! She could feel herself starting to blush and the tumult of all the emotion just made her mad.

"What are you doing here, Tim?" came out of nowhere, like the bark of a rabid dog. She was confused by her own venom, and judging by the look on his face, so was he. It wasn't at all what she had been hoping for.

"Well, good morning to you too, princess. I wasn't sure how it was going to be, seeing you this morning, but I guess it's like this, again. It's too bad, really. I don't know why you are afraid of me, or mad at me, if that's what it is... but I said I was going to see you today, and I meant it. I really couldn't think of anything else. I thought maybe I could buy you a coffee, since I spilled the last one we shared together."

Monica panicked. She didn't think she could sit calmly across a table from him, she didn't really think she could sit calmly anywhere with him. She felt the panic happen; her skin got hot, her hands started flailing, and her cheeks burned. She couldn't mess this one up. "Please. Please, don't take me out for coffee, I can't handle being with you in public right now."

Tim stepped back. He repeated the words carefully. "You can't be with me in public? Is that what you just said?"

Monica watched his reaction in slow motion, she could feel the heat on her top lip; this was going a thousand percent wrong. She had to do something to keep him from leaving! She stepped up to a very confused-looking Tim, grabbed his face and pulled it to her, kissing him slowly and tenderly. After a startled initial reaction from him, she felt a deep sigh, and his whole body seemed to relax. Her hands moved to wrap around his body and pressed into the small of his back, pulling him to her even more securely.

Tim's eyebrows rose for a second, and then, in a few steps, he was pushing her against the wall of her office building, pressing her right up onto her toes. The entire tempo of the kiss changed, and Monica was on fire. Tim grabbed her chin and tipped it up, and began to nuzzle her neck, licking and nipping her skin down to her collarbone. Her breath started coming faster. She could hear him humming, almost growling.

"Inside, inside." Monica could barely think but knew the world did not need to see her being ravaged outside her workplace. Tim's eyebrows were almost invisible. "Oh my god. Tim. Get us inside. I have a sofa, and a door to close. Please?"

Tim released her back down to the ground but ran his hands around her back to cup her ass and pull her even closer to him. He whispered, "If this is how you act when you are mad at me, Mon, I'm going to do everything I can to keep you mad. You got that? Monica, I've been planning what to do to you since last night. I couldn't even sleep. I need to see all of you."

Monica shuddered, her entire body completely ready to let him have her then and there. She didn't trust herself to speak and cleared her throat, grabbing his arm and leading him to the office. As she unlocked the front door, he began gently tracing his fingers along her collarbone. He ran his finger under her blouse and under the strap of her bra, easing it over her shoulder. "I'm sure this is very pretty, but I cannot wait to see it on the floor."

Monica's eyes felt heavy with lust, like they were shutting down. She fumbled with the key and hardly managed to get the door open. One more door, she thought. Just one more. She moved fast down the hallway, feeling him touching her along the way. A light touch on her back, a finger run along the curve of her ass. His hands were on her the whole time. The last door was opened, and locked behind her, and she dashed for her personal office. The last thing she needed was her assistant to find her on the floor of the office with a man. She made it in, with Tim immediately behind her, and closed the door. She let out a deep sigh of relief. Public exposure would not be a problem after all. They were finally safe behind a closed door. He was finally not touching her, and she turned to look at him.

"Last chance to back out, Monnie. You really okay with this? I'm a vasectomy man, in case that helps." Tim had his arms crossed and was looking anywhere but at her. She could see the substantial bulge in his pants clearly. *Oh my god, it was huge! And it had been a long, long time.* She stepped toward him.

"If you don't fuck me, I swear to God, I will fuck you up."

Tim let out a slow laugh, stepped toward her and pushed her up against her just-closed office door.

"Well, all right then, if you put it that way, Princess." Monica closed her eyes.

Tim pulled Monica's arms above her head, placed his thigh between hers, and pressed her back against the door. He tugged her blouse out from her skirt and slipped it down her shoulders, exposing her breasts. He looked down at her breasts in their lace bra, "Ah, I've seen this bra before, at the coffeeshop… and I've dreamed of doing this ever since." He pulled the bra down, releasing her breasts, one into each of his hands. He had his thumbs on each nipple, rubbing them slowly. Monica reached back to unhook the clasp, and Tim lowered his mouth to her nipples, licking and nipping at her until she gasped. The bra dropped to the floor, and Tim looked up at her, his eyes darkened with lust. Monica slid her hands down his shoulders and around his waist, tugging his shirt out and lifting it over his head so she could feel more of his skin.

As she peeled the shirt from his shoulders, she caught sight of a large, black, almost tribal tattoo on his chest. A Bear paw print; not cute, not cuddly, complete with claws. It was the size of her own hand. She rested her hand on it; it was beautifully done, and so simple. His skin was hot and smooth, and she tangled her fingers in the hair that he had at the base of his neck. "Oh God, you are beautiful, Tim, so damn hot."

Tim threw his head back and laughed outright. "Ain't seen nothing yet, babe." He began to flick her nipples with his thumbs, again, still holding her up against the door. The sensations began to build for Monica, the heat between her legs exacerbated by Tim's thigh pressing against her, holding her up high against the door. She started rubbing her pussy back and forth on Tim's thigh as he flicked her nipples. Tim growled a little as she began to move. He gave her nipples a solid tweak before he reached around her and lifted her against him. Her legs went around his middle and her breasts rested on his chest, further inflaming her nipples. Tim spun and brought her to rest down on her back on the sofa in the office. His voice was husky and deep as he said, "I need us both to be naked, right now."

Monica nodded, slipped her fingers under her skirt's

waistband, and slid the whole thing down, panties and all. Her legs went up as she slid them over her toes, and Tim grabbed her ankles. "Keep these up here," he grunted.

Monica's eyes were at his thighs, and she had to look up to see his face. She hadn't seen such fierceness before, not with a man simply looking at her body. She felt like she was about to be devoured. It made her quiver with anticipation. She was ready for it, wet as she'd ever been. She slid her hand over the warm bulge at his crotch. "Get naked, Tim. Let me see you."

Tim held her ankles up with one hand, undid his pants with the other, and released his cock from constriction.

Monica gave a little gasp. "Tim. You're fucking beautiful. Oh my god." Tim's cock was thick and hard, and Tim leaned right in to give it to Monica's waiting mouth. She wrapped her hand around his shaft and licked him up and down. Tim's legs shook.

He ran his hand down her legs while he held them up, coming to rest on her hot pussy. He rubbed his thumb on her clit briefly before sliding two fingers into her waiting wetness. Monica held on to his cock but arched her back at the sensation.

"My God, you are so wet, lady. I think you've been needing me." He stepped away from her side, and she let her fingers slide down his length as he went. He stepped out of his jeans, and she watched his ass. *His body was fucking perfect,* she thought. *Unbelievable. Not an extra pound on him and chiseled in all the places.* He climbed onto the sofa, on his knees, his cock erect and inches from her pussy, her legs still up in the air, knees together. He pulled her legs to him, resting her calves on his shoulders. Monica could hardly stand that her pussy was so close to his cock. She angled her pelvis up to rub her juices on his shaft.

Tim closed his eyes. "Monica," he whispered, "I can't. I

want to take my time, but I can't. I need to be in you, right fucking now." Monica lay back and opened her legs, sliding them off his shoulders, opening for him in the greatest permission. She couldn't wait either.

Tim grabbed his cock and rested the tip on the lips of her pussy. He dipped into the entrance, feeling its heat and smoothness. Monica's head was back, her back was arching. She let out a little whimper and that was it, his last piece of control broke. He plunged in.

He filled Monica entirely, and she loved it. She smiled to herself as he thrust, angling her body to get him in still deeper. Tim sighed an enormous sigh. This felt so right. She felt right with him. He fit her so well, and his thrusts were already starting to speed up. She took him, her legs pulling him in as she wrapped around him. "Tim, I want you to... I want you to fuck me like an animal. Fuck me hard. Come on. Do it. Don't hold back."

It was all Tim could bear. He grabbed her thighs and drove into her. Again and again and again. Monica couldn't think. It was a fucking miracle.

She reached a hand down and started to rub her clit. She was ready to cum and could only believe Tim was going to match her. He looked down and saw her circling, and he got even deeper. His eyes were dark as he lost himself. The sounds he was making were growls and grunts. Monica loved it. He plunged all the way in, and she threw her hands back as he pounded on her pussy. She could feel herself squeezing him. Her whole body was arching. He looked completely out of control as he came, and his orgasm was so powerful his entire body froze. Monica was still moving below him and was no longer able to think. She could feel her pussy pulsing on him as he started to come back down to Earth, and her climax threw her head back and she screamed into the side of the sofa. Her whole body convulsed, and she felt her pussy tightening on his still hard cock. She felt hot liquid squirting from herself, soaking his shaft and he fell forward on her body, sweat-slicked and panting.

Monica was panting too. She was quickly trying to remember if she'd ever orgasmed with just a penis before. She didn't think so; it had always been with toys or fingers or tongues. *Fuck.* "That was fucking amazing, Tim," she gasped.

Tim stayed inside her a minute more, then slid out of her and worked his way around to be behind her on the sofa. He held her in his enormous arms, resting his thigh on her hip. He brushed the hair out of her face and nuzzled the back of her head. "You are so goddamned amazing, Monnie. Your eyes have the most amazing sparks in them, it's like fireworks in there. I want to lick you everywhere and take little bites as I go."

Monica had never had anyone do anything like this, talking and continuing the love making, after the sex. Her ex had been big on rolling over and going to sleep once he came. Tim was love-listing her body parts from toes to hair, and it was amazing, and made her feel like six billion dollars. He even liked the smell of her sweat. She sighed in his arms and snuggled a little closer, if it was even possible on this sofa, made tiny by Tim's substantial frame.

They talked, asking questions of each other. Tim shared that all of his brothers, and even some friends, had the Bear claw tattoo, reminding her that they'd called themselves the Bear Clan way back in Elementary School, and it had stuck. She talked a little about her ex, and about her design company. Eventually, they separated and got ready for the rest of their day. They had a long, lingering kiss at the doorway to her office, and they both smiled as they said goodbye, for now.

CHAPTER 8

Tim definitely had a spring in his step and the loveliest of tight muscles in his glutes. Every step he took reminded him of thrusting into Monica, holding her hips as he pounded her. She'd loved it! Being able to tell just blew him away. Terri had always just taken it; she had barely looked at him. It had begun to feel like he was alone, and their sex life had just drifted away. Fucking Monica had felt so right, so damn satisfying. He was late for work, but he definitely did not care. He was not going to think about Terri at all today. He was going into The Cup to pick up his Cuban and an Americano for Alice. She would've texted him if he'd needed to be in earlier.

He walked in to find Max huddled up with Bill behind the counter. Surprised, he called out to them, "What's up?"

Max and Bill looked up and gestured to him to join. They moved back deeper into the kitchen, out of view of the customers.

"Good timing, Tim," said Bill. "You know, when I saw you last night, nothing had been worth noting? Well, that sure as hell changed."

Tim's eyebrows went up. "We found four sets of clothes out there, all piled up nice and neat for some shifters to return to. They don't belong to any of us, and no one has come back to claim them today."

Tim's eyebrows climbed into his hairline. "I'm assuming you've been watching?"

Max leaned in, nodding. "The only animals good enough to spot a Bear hiding in wait are Wolves. It's Wolves. I have no doubt. I went out after Bill called me this morning and could smell them all over town. They haven't come back for their clothes because they are staying Wolves, and they know that we are watching now. If they stay Wolves for too long, they'll be feral, and we cannot have four feral Wolves here or anywhere near here."

"What's Harriet got to say?" Tim asked. Harriet was Max's family, though not biological. Their parents had adopted a slew of kids over the years, most with a shifter story or a connection to the magic of the world.

"Harriet's out there talking to Red," grumbled Max. "They're always full of things to say to each other. I can't believe they don't run out. I've called her over here at least twice."

Tim looked out the window and over at Harriet, sitting close by Wendy with the gorgeous auburn hair. They were the very picture of best friends, smiling and laughing at their conversation. Tim raised his hands and gave a piercing whistle. Everyone in The Cup startled and looked up. Harriet got up from her seat, whispered one more thing to Wendy, and headed over to Tim. Wendy's eyes were big and she wore a faint, slightly nervous smile.

Max took a step back, seeing as how he knew already what was coming. Harriet walked into the kitchen and stalked directly up to Tim. She took a deep breath, looked up at him and said calmly but in a stone-cold chill, "Tim. Tim.

You ever call me like a dog again, anywhere, *anywhere* ... I will personally set your pubic hair on fire, permanently. Do we understand each other?"

It was Tim's turn to step back. "Yes ma'am, sorry Harriet."

"Just so we're clear. What is so goddamn important I can't talk to my friend on my one break per month?" Harriet spun to all of them.

"There's Wolves in town, Harriet," Max said in a low voice. "At least four, and they can't shift right now because we're watching their clothes."

Harriet straightened up. She rolled her shoulders and stretched her neck like she was readying for a fight. "Okay. Bill, Tim, get the Bears together. We need more than patrolling, right now. Max, if you can, I want you to track them down. We need to know where they've been, what they've been watching, and if they've left town. I'm going to go call the Tribunal and see if last summer's rogue Wolf has anything to help us. Meet back here at 5."

Harriet left the kitchen, talked to Wendy for a few minutes more, and went out the front door. Wendy was pulling on an apron as Tim, Bill, and Max followed behind. She gave a shy wave as they headed out.

CHAPTER 9

*H*arriet and the shifters all met back at The Cup at 5, as Wendy was wiping down tables and flipping the Open sign to Closed. She grabbed Max's arm as he came by and whispered details about the afternoon before waving again as she slid out the door. Max looked bemused as he joined the group. "Remind me to do the coffee machines, Harriet."

Harriet nodded and began the meeting. "Okay, the Wolf from last year that we've got at the Council is messed up. Deeply messed up, like his brain is not working right. He's no help to us with this new development. Max, what'd you find?"

Max leaned forward, "I tracked two Wolves' paths across town; they came by here, went down past the library, hit the strip by the Bouncy Hut, and seemed to head back into the woods behind the Town Hall. The other two seemed more erratic, the paths were separate, and I couldn't tell them apart from each other. I couldn't begin to tell you where they ended up."

"What do you mean, seemed, when you say they 'seemed' to head back into the woods? Can't you tell if they left?" Bill asked Max.

"No," said Max. "I can't tell you that they didn't come back in. I stopped tracking them at that point, as I wanted to follow the other paths before they dissipated."

"Okay," sighed Harriet. "Bill, if you can, will you double up on the patrols in the woods around town? I just think a strong scent presence would be good, right now. Wolves are notorious for their scent aversion, and Bears, you guys stink like nobody's business," she smiled.

Bill and Tim both smiled back. "Proud of it," laughed Tim. "Bill, I'll get the boys out of the trucks now. We'll head out behind Alice's, first, so we can leave our stuff in the back. Okay?"

"Yeah, good, go. Thanks, Tim." Bill leaned over to Max once Tim was out the door. "Is there anything going on, Max? Why do *you* think we've got four Wolves visiting? Is it possible they're harmless?"

Max ran his hands through his hair. "I don't know, man. If they're from my old pack, they're not harmless. But with what Harriet is saying about the mind of the Wolf we found, I really don't know what this could be."

"Harriet, what're you finding with him? What's going on?" Bill leaned back to hear from Harriet.

"If I didn't feel so crazy saying this, I'd think he'd been brainwashed or something. Bill, I've got no idea what's wrong with him, but he's not responding to any of the treatments we've been trying. They can't get him to say anything beyond Max's pack name." Harriet ran her own hands through her hair; an unconscious family trait she shared with Max and all their adoptive siblings.

"Okay, let's at least figure out if they're still here. Max, can you close up? I'm going to go with Bill out to Alice's and see what I can sense of the woods from there," Harriet said. Max nodded and they all left The Cup for the last time that day.

CHAPTER 10

Monica had a full, long, and busy day at the office, but she felt like she was floating the whole time. She could feel her pussy was swollen from all the pounding she'd gotten, and it was a very happy ache. *Oh my god, how can I forget how great that was, ever?* Every time she touched herself or tugged her skirt down, she thought of Tim and his arms and chest and the Bear claw tattoo. Her muscles were sore and every part of her was just a little more relaxed.

She was getting ready to head out to get the boys from her brother and get her mom-work evening started. The kids were starting school next week and needed to start getting back into a routine. She drove her neighbor's giant Caddy over to the Bouncy Hut and noticed what looked like a vagrant in the alley as she passed. *In Mossy Ridge? A vagrant?* How was that even possible? They had great social services here in town and nobody fell through the net, ever. But still, it was enough of an unsettling sight to have her walk a little quicker after she parked and when she went to get the kids. She felt like she was back in the city for a minute. Fast walk with the purse under the arm and the keys in the fingers? Check.

Luke and Brian were fine; they were sweaty and exhausted and full of pizza. Frank had fed them again, giving her another much-needed break from the 'What's for dinner' debacle. Frank was a true godsend. After their crap childhood, Frank had stayed meek, and Monica was tough as nails on the outside, and they both had figured out how to cope, kind of. Monica was so glad to have Frank around while exhausted by her quasi-frantic worry. He was the only man that she trusted, and she would do anything for him. She knew he'd do the same. It was good to have someone know her, to see her soft and squishy side and not take advantage of it. She was so organized and brilliant at getting the boys everywhere on time; she was a scheduling ninja. But when it came to food? Everyone was happy as long as something hit the plates, is how she felt about it. They ate a lot of scrambled eggs. Breakfast for dinner was where it was at for her.

* * *

SHE THOUGHT ABOUT TIM a fair amount as the evening went on. *Should I call him? Are we at calling level? Is it a one-time thing? Am I going to see him again? Had he liked being with me?* That one made her laugh. If there was one thing a man could not fake, it was that. Her brain was acting like a teenager's, with all the uncertainty and self-doubt involved. Well, her pussy was acting up too, for that matter. She was getting wet just thinking about it. *Was I supposed to call him? Was he supposed to call me?*

The boys were sleeping, and she was sitting with her tea in the kitchen, looking over the meeting notes of the day. A text came in from Tim. Just a simple 'Thinking of you.' She couldn't help but smile a big, satisfied smile, in the middle of the kitchen.

The next text to come in was an eggplant and a peach. Monica laughed out loud at the innuendo-laden images. She typed back "You are an animal, Tim. I've been thinking of you, too."

They texted images to each other for a while, and then, the phone actually rang. Monica was startled by the sound in her quiet kitchen and connected automatically, without looking. It was Tim.

"Monica? I didn't mean to scare you by actually calling, but it's me, Tim. I want to invite you out on an official date, with clothes on and everything." Tim laughed. "I want to get this started the right way. Dinner tomorrow, if you're free and can get a sitter?"

Monica was flustered and caught off guard by the formality of the phone call and the richness of his voice. "Oh! Okay, Tim … I'm going to have to get back to you, I'm not sure I can get a sitter that quick. Let me call Animal, I mean, Alice. I'll get back to you." She disconnected weirdly and quickly. Hearing his voice brought back some of the tender, new feelings she had when he'd been smoothing back her hair that morning. *It was just this morning!* She shook her head in bewilderment.

What was going on? What was this? A Lawson? Really? Was she going to actually date a Lawson? She didn't even know if she wanted to text Alice about it. Then Alice would know something about her business. This wasn't how she wanted to be seen in this town.

She was an independent, powerful woman who everyone called a bitch. She knew how they talked about her, but she didn't care. She made choices for the best of the community and for her family, period. She'd be damned if she did anything else. She'd come right up against the Lawson's on the Town Council and they were always trying to make changes, to make trouble, just like in high school.

Monica's brain was racing. She was still feeling the effects of the surprise lovemaking, and it was mixing in with practicality and common sense of her life. The mix was unpleasant and made her stomach feel queasy now. Dating? How would the boys take that? They'd been fine with the separation and looming divorce because she was with them full time. How would it be if there was someone around? *What the hell was she thinking?! It had just been sex! That's all!*

Monica took a deep breath. "Holy shit. I'm losing my fucking mind. Time to go to bed, Monica."

* * *

TIM GOT OFF THE PHONE AND FELT A LITTLE INSECURE. HE hadn't really liked that 'You're an animal' comment, but she didn't know he was a shifter, so what could he say? Was it on her mind that something was wrong about him? Tim knew she was super smart but couldn't believe she'd suspect that there were animal shifters in the world, never mind that Tim was one. Monica's abrupt shift from funny emoji friend to curt, practical phone mistress was pretty drastic. He hadn't known quite what to do, and she'd ended the phone call before he'd had any chance to respond. Was this the venom coming back? Had something happened between morning and night? Or between texts? What was wrong with this woman? Was she always so mercurial?

He'd been out most of the day with the Bears, making up new patrol schedules and following Max as he sniffed out new tracks or tried to find the route the Wolves may have taken. The alley by the Bouncy Hut had been really well-visited, it seemed. Max couldn't sort out what had gone on there, just that there had been a strong Wolf presence. Tim was tired, and really disappointed that he'd gone from laughing and teasing with Monica to feeling bewildered and deflated. Billy was already in bed, and Tim was heading up himself, again, and alone.

He was rattled out of his self-pity by a large clatter from outside. He peered out his back window, expecting to see a raccoon in the trash cans. What he saw instead, chilled him to the bone. A large gray Wolf was sitting at the edge of the woods in his back yard. Any full human would have missed him, but the Bear's eyes picked out the size and shape of the Wolf immediately. Tim gasped and turned to race down the stairs.

By the time he got to the yard, the Wolf was gone. He had phone in hand and was texting the entire Bear pack, and Max. Max arrived first, and stood quietly at the edge of the yard with Tim.

"I just, I just feel like this is all about me," said Max, "like, I've brought this danger into Mossy Ridge, and I can't stand it, Tim. I just can't stand it. I've got to go, *now.*"

"Max, I understand, I really do. But you need to wait for backup. Just a few more minutes, I promise. You're part of our pack now, and this is when it matters, right now. Bears are solitary, but when we need to protect our range, our families, we do it together. You're one of us, and we back you up, all the way. We can't back you up if you head off alone."

Within minutes, multiple cars were pulling into the driveway.

Max sighed and turned back toward Tim. His eyes went wide as he saw the dozens of Bear shifters getting out of their cars and coming into the yard. "I didn't even know there were so many, Tim."

"Bill put out an emergency call, Max. You've probably never seen it happen before. I think I've only seen it once, when a cub was lost in the 80's. Some of these Bears, I haven't seen since I was a kid."

Bill strode up to Max, put his hand on his shoulder, and turned to face the assembled crowd. It was pitch black, but many sets of eyes reflected the lights of the house. "Bears, we're here because a Wolf has been seen. This Wolf was in our brother, Tim's, yard here and ran North into the woods. We've found clothing stashes this week and traces of scent all over town. We know there are at least four, and we need to get our hands on at least one of these Wolves, find out what the story is. We are not on attack; we are on reconnaissance and removal. Should there be reason, use the force you deem necessary, but we need to find out *why* the Wolves are here. We're breaking the woods into sectors to search. See Mike for your section. Head out as soon as you know. Meet back here at dawn, or signal if you find something. Good hunting."

The air was crackling with the tension of all the shifters. The crowd dispersed after swirling around Mike. Max got his assignment and took off. Tim and Bill were paired to go up the hills and around back to check on Alice's neck of the woods. The air was full of shimmers as the men and women shifted into the animals within them. Tim and Bill loped off into the woods, moving as quickly and as quietly as Bears can.

The woods were quiet; most of the nocturnal animals knew that something was going on, and the usual chitter and chirp was silenced. Bill and Tim moved down the slope toward Alice's home, scanning left and right as they went. They stopped at the edge of the woods, looking toward the house. Alice was talking softly on the phone on the back porch. Bill gave an appreciative growl at the sight of her. She looked up and squinted into the woods, but they were too far back to be seen, and she must have doubted her hearing, because she continued her murmured conversation and went back into the house.

Something crackled off to Bill's left, and he pivoted quickly. The two Bears froze at the sight of a man lying naked not 100 feet from them. He was curled into the fetal position and looked as if he'd been naked for days, he was so covered in filth. Tim quickly shifted back into human form and took the sweatpants and t-shirt from the pack he always kept at Alice's woods – they all had packs of clothes at Alice's. There was a perfect lean-to about 100 yards out from the house. It was a deeply practical solution for shifters who turn up naked after a shift.

Tim quickly dressed and slowly approached the naked man. Bill growled a deeply threatening growl. "Bill, I want him to wake up to a human, okay? We need to keep him human so we can hear what he's got to say. Go get a blanket or something from Alice, and some rope to tie him up so he can't shift."

Bill got the materials he needed and then some. Alice came out and she and Bill wiped some of the worst filth from the man and tied him in a way that would inhibit his ability to shift. He wasn't entirely conscious but moaned and muttered from time to time. Bill brought his truck around and they proceeded to move the operation to Bill's house. Harriet and Max met them there. Max looked shocked at the sight of the man.

"I know him! He was one of the more powerful Wolves in the old pack. He was fair; he wasn't one of the worst. I can't begin to imagine how he got like this."

Harriet made some phone calls and drove off with the Wolf-man and some of the other Bears in the back of her truck.

Bill told Tim to call it quits for the night. There'd been no other sightings or scents to track, and dawn was underway.

Once everyone was squared away, Tim headed back to the house. He walked into the house to find his neighbor and Billy fast asleep together on the sofa, with cartoons blaring in front of them. Tim smiled and woke up the neighbor and sent her home. She knew all about the shifters in town and was always available for emergencies. It was really nice that some people knew. It took some of the pressure off by not needing to keep the 'big secret' all the time. Tim wondered if Monica knew anything about the shifters in town. He highly doubted it. But it was entirely possible, either way, that she knew everything or that she didn't know shifters existed. It was complicated. Would it ever be okay to tell someone you were dating that you could turn into an animal at any given moment?

It had been wonderful that Terri had always known. Terri was a shifter too. But it had never really been right with Terri. For all the drama and heartache that he had felt when she left, there was a large part of him that had not been surprised at all. And there was a tiny, tiny sliver in himself that had been relieved when she finally left. Relieved. Taking time to heal from the abandonment had meant recognizing that relief as a sign that he had known all along it wasn't right. And his Bear had certainly shown more interest and compulsion around Monica than he'd ever felt for Terri.

But what *about* Monica? Did she know? Could he just keep going along as he was and not ever tell her? It wasn't as if it was forever. Tim's mind tripped over that thought a little. And then again. Did he want it to be forever? His Bear growled in satisfaction. *Woah!* Tim just couldn't handle the questions and feelings the thoughts were bringing up. *Monica? It was Monica?* Telling Monica he was a shifter did not mean he had to stay with her forever. Hiding it from her wasn't anything more than a thought for convenience and simplicity. Right? What would she say when she found out?

Would she stay? Would she run away? Would those green eyes be disgusted with him? Would he ever see her beautiful breasts in his hands again? He didn't want to imagine the possibility that she would reject him. But she sure could.

A piece of Tim's Bear seemed pretty damn satisfied that Tim had moved into this line of questioning. Tim really wasn't sure about Monica, but the Bear sure damn was.

CHAPTER 11

*T*he next morning, Monica woke up full of doubts. *A date? A real date? Like, what people do when they want to be in relationships? Relationships that end up breaking you into little bits and leaving you sobbing in the bathtub?* She was tired and couldn't make sense of her feelings or what she wanted to do about Tim. She'd had sex dreams *and* anxiety dreams, and it was all just awful. In her dreams, she was shouting at herself that Tim was an animal but at least he wasn't her ex. She hadn't slept well, and she woke up thinking about her ex and why he had never loved her. Her filter was long gone, and she groaned loudly as she held her head in her hands. Her boys looked at each other over the breakfast table and laughed in their hands when Monica was looking away.

Luke turned to Brian, "We have the coolest mom, Brian. You'll know it more when you get older, like me." Brian just turned his wide, mirth-filled eyes on his empty cereal bowl.

"Oh, damn it, guys, I'm sorry. I'm just all messed up in my brain right now. What cereal do you want today?" She needed to get a handle back on the day; groaning at the boys over breakfast was not her idea of a good plan. Monica got ready for work. It was Friday Fun Day and the last one before the boys started school. Dinner was their choice and they always chose the same thing, so she was ready. Chicken wings and a movie, after bowling. *Ah!* Actually, remembering that gave her the answer to the Tim dilemma. She couldn't have a real date; it was Friday Fun Day. Boom. She texted him from the bedroom, immediately, and it was done. And she didn't have to feel guilty because kids came first! She felt her shoulders drop for the first time that morning.

She hadn't realized how stressed she'd been about trying to decide about Tim. He was just a guy, after all. Plenty of people 'just had sex' and were still upstanding people. She was pretty sure she wasn't those people, but she liked him. I mean, he was gorgeous, so utterly fine that she couldn't always breathe right around him. That was fine, right? She vaguely wondered what the big deal was as she headed out to finally get her car back from the shop. The car guys would return the Caddy to her neighbor, Miss Crocker, for her, as she was so-and-so's great aunt or something. Win-Win for small town connections.

She sat down at her desk a little while later and began to go over the proposals before the Council for the next week. Usually, it was just a browse through but this week, there were several proposals that were going to affect the traffic around the center of Mossy Ridge. Her brother's Bouncy Hut was there, and several other businesses that would not want to be impacted by gross traffic increases. She saw the name Mathewson on one of the documents and sat back. "That goddamn horrible cow," she said, then looked around to make sure no one could have heard. Mrs. Mathewson was a little bit famous in Mossy Ridge.

Mrs. Mathewson had several boys who'd slummed their way through Mossy Ridge's public schools, after getting booted from their posh private schools, all of them for different infractions. She was a notoriously difficult woman and had raised, along with 'the help', several terrible people. She owned several large parcels of land around town, one of which abutted several of the businesses in the center of Mossy Ridge. Monica couldn't believe the Mathewson Project was really moving ahead. Mrs. Mathewson had been trying to get it developed for years and had always come afoul of some zoning law, or she'd made her own trouble. It had happened more than once that Mrs. Mathewson had fired entire crews of workers for being 'late' or 'messy'.

Who got suckered into this one? Ahhh. Ursa Development. That was Tim's brother's company. Sigh.

Tim. He'd pushed his fingers into her pussy right here in this room. He'd held her legs up and made her feel so damn hot, right on that sofa. She could almost still smell the sex. She'd been so crazed for him, so wildly turned on, that anything could've happened and it, really, mostly did. She sat back in her chair and gave herself a few minutes to remember. She could feel her nipples hardening and her pussy getting wet. Hot damn, that guy was so hot. His arms were so strong, and his chest! Oh god, and that cock? It was unreal, like comic book hero style. He looked so mild-mannered and brainy when he was wearing clothes. But oh my god! The Bear claw tattoo was usually not her style, but on him, it was perfect, somehow. And mild-mannered he was, but not when naked. Hallelujah. He was like Clark Kent and Superman at once, and shoot, she just couldn't believe her luck.

Focus, Monica. She took a deep breath and stretched her neck. She looked through the proposal for the land and it was intriguing but would certainly bring a fair amount of change. It was so intriguing that she had a slight suspicion that Mrs. Mathewson wasn't entirely aware of it. A slew of small, single-family homes, with some slated for low-income applicants? Yeah, that didn't really seem like Mrs. Mathewson's style. She'd send her a quick note. It was always good to have everything on the table. Everyone had to be on the same page, or the project would just get tossed, eventually.

The rest of the projects looked fine, thankfully, and the day wound down. She didn't get any response from Tim, which was a little strange, but she was busy, and it was a niggle but not a nudge in the back of her mind. She packed up, looked back to be sure the office looked good, and noticed the rumple on the sofa where she and Tim had been.

Oh my god, what a great story that was. I so wish I could have more. What? Woah. Where had that thought come from? Focus! Time to go home, Friday Fun Day, remember? Monica smiled to herself and closed the door to the office and headed home.

CHAPTER 12

Tim had gotten the text from Monica but hadn't gotten it till mid-afternoon. He'd caught up on the missed night of sleep while little Billy played with Alice's kids. Alice was a godsend, for sure. She knew the men had all missed sleep and had offered to take all the kids, all at once. He assumed it was a circus over there, but Big Bill was sleeping on his sofa currently, and Tim was moving slowly around the house, getting ready for the day, finally. The text was mildly confusing, but Tim assumed it was a brushoff of some kind and he'd been too busy to be offended. Her attitude on the phone was weird enough to make anything probable. Something about kids and fun bowling?

He really owed Alice for the sleep he'd been able to get. Between last night and Billy's whole life, he felt like he needed about a month of sleep to get back to normal human levels. He had the absurd idea that coffee was actually in his blood at this point, and that he'd be a zombie without it. He was brewing some now and could hear Bill moving around in the living room.

"Coffee?" he called.

"Please," Bill answered, somewhat muffled. He came into the kitchen, still pulling a sweatshirt over his head.

"Alice is a flipping god-send, Bill. I can't believe she took all the kids for the day. She just saved half the shifters in this town from becoming zombies for a few days, especially me. I'm going to thank her, but please make sure you tell her how amazing she is… Flowers, maybe?"

Bill sighed. "I can't believe it either, Tim. She just keeps getting better. From knowing nothing about shifters to the way she supports us all now? I could never have imagined something like it. I'm the luckiest man in the world."

Tim thought instantly of Monica. *Could she possibly handle it?* His Bear grumbled at him. "How did you tell her, Bill? How could anyone accommodate the truth of shifters? Did she freak out?"

Bill looked at Tim strangely. "She freaked out, shut me out, and then, slowly, opened the door. It was scary, for both of us. It doesn't matter how strong a shifter you are, you have to let them sort it out for themselves, and its awful to wait, just awful. If its right, its right. Something happening that I don't know about, Tim? You have someone you need to tell, Tim?"

Tim looked down. "No, just thinking about it. It was never an issue with Terri, obviously, but she couldn't handle the parenting instead. I guess I'd rather have someone struggle with my being a Bear inside than struggle with responsibility." He gave a weak laugh.

Bill put his hand on Tim's shoulder. "Forgive me for saying so, again, Tim, but Terri was a flat-out irresponsible bitch. I mean, marriages fail and all, but what kind of person leaves their kid?! Who knows what kind of weakness she had in her, but it was obvious, to all of us, that she wasn't in it for the right reasons. We had hoped she'd grow out of it. But there are many more fish in the sea, and strong women are all around us. Just look for one, if you're ready. Whoever you pick will be able to handle it, with a little time."

With that, Bill drained his coffee and left to help Alice with the kids. Tim followed, after a shower and a snack. When he arrived, all the kids were gone but Billy, and Alice's own. Alice looked a little haggard but was still smiling and passing out popcorn.

"How would you like to do some bowling tonight, guys? All of you, yeah. I heard they even serve pizza, unless you're completely over pizza now," Tim said with a wink.

All three shrieked. Alice looked at Tim, "You sure you can handle all three?"

Tim scoffed. "I'm a pro now, Alice, remember? Plus, your two make Billy the easiest kid in the world, and it'll be a pretty early night, honestly, it's just bowling. You need a little break. You made today so much smoother by taking all the kids. You deserve a million dollars, but all I can do is buy pizza and rent bowling shoes. Let me. Please?"

Bill moved in and took the popcorn out of her hands and kissed her on the forehead. Alice nodded, and Tim and the kids took off to the bowling lanes.

CHAPTER 13

The kids ran in ahead of him as he walked through the mostly empty parking lot. Thankful it wasn't league night, he was actually looking forward to letting the kids loose inside. He already heard their squeals of joy as the doors closed on them when they entered. God bless the other people inside. He could imagine a pretty fun night ahead. The kids were so good together, and it was always fulfilling to watch Billy have fun. He was glad to be able to do something for Alice too. It felt good to return the favor.

He couldn't help but think it was a great benefit for Billy, to see how older kids behaved, to have a role model like an older sibling could give, like Bill was to him. He really admired how Bill ran the Bear clan with the other shifters, and how fair and reliable he was. Bill had been an amazing source of support when Terri ran off. Tim remember the shock and confusion he'd felt that day, walking into the house in disarray, the closets empty and some of the furniture taken. She must have been planning it for a while.

He'd picked up little Billy at daycare – he was just a little bitty thing then – and headed home. The driveway had been empty and the front door ajar. Tim left Billy asleep in his car seat and went to check it out. He moved slowly into the house, his Bear at the surface, listening and smelling for danger. There was nothing, just an empty house. There was a note on the table in Terri's handwriting, but Tim couldn't bear to open it. Tim got Billy and brought him in. Then, he called Bill.

Bill arrived in minutes and took the note from Tim's hands at the door. His eyes scanned it, getting wider as he read. He put his hand on Tim's shoulder, and with eyes brimming with tears, said, "She's gone, Tim. She left. She has surrendered Billy to you entirely. She doesn't say anything more than 'I can't handle this anymore. I have to go live my own life. Take care of the punk for me. You're a better parent already than I'll ever be.'"

Tim and Billy had spent the night at Bill's. Tim couldn't face the empty house, the echoes, the loss. He felt like Terri was going to walk around the corner any minute, that it was all some kind of bad dream. When they'd eventually gone back, a week or so later, he found that Bill and his brothers had cleaned the house up, spread his clothes out in the closet and they'd even moved the sofa around, to give him a change of scenery. Mike and Curt were coming in the next week to paint the bathroom with a mural for Billy. Tim could never thank his family enough. It had made all the difference in his healing; though, he still found it easy to fall into an occasional rage about Terri. He'd never put himself in a position to be walked out on again. He sighed as he got ready to go inside and just be Dad again.

He pulled open the doors of the Lanes to see Monica's curvy ass just inside. His cock recognized it. She was leaning over the counter, reaching for something. "Monica?" he asked, surprised.

She turned to him, startled. He watched her face go

through what he was beginning to recognize as 'Monica's emotions'.

"Yeah, Tim, stalk much?" Monica spit.

Tim stepped back. It was venomous Monica today. Shoot. He did some quick thinking. *Stalking? What?* Ohhh, damn, now he remembered. He would actually need to explain this one. "Oh my god, no, Monica. I mean, not really. I got your message, and it must've implanted the bowling idea. I forgot you were going to be here. I'm … we're not going to bother you, I swear. We'll get a lane at the other end of the place, I promise. It was a total accident." He was so desperate to explain himself that he could hear the pleading in his voice. Ugh. He stood up a little straighter. It was not as if he was going to beg Monica to take his kid bowling. What the hell?

He watched Monica start to soften. Her stance relaxed, and she took a deep breath.

"Crap. Tim, I'm sorry. I'm not used to sharing Friday Fun Days and I think I was nervous that you really were showing up here on purpose. There's no reason for that, I get it. The boys will actually love to have more kids here. They are tired of me beating them," she laughed. "We could share lane space, even."

Tim relaxed. He leaned in close enough to smell her hair. He took a deep breath of her scent. "Okay, Monica. Let's hang out with a million kids. It'll be easy, I promise. I won't even take your clothes off, or anything."

Monica glanced around quickly. "Tim!"

"Well, I'm not going to pretend that nothing happened between us, Mon. I love how you smell, and I remember all of it. Even if I don't talk about it, you need to know I'm going to always be aware of it … your body, and how your pussy squeezed me. I want you right now, here, in exactly the same way I had you before."

Monica looked up at him. He just nodded and went to get

shoes for the kids, who were running wild in the arcade, coinless. Monica stood stunned for a minute, remembering it all, before shaking it off and following.

They had a really nice night, full of laughs and kid-centered goofiness. Monica and Tim sat together and watched the big kids try to teach Billy how to use the full-sized bowling ball. It was hysterical, as Billy could barely pick it up, and almost rolled down the lane with it when it finally went.

* * *

As the night wore on, and the kids started getting tired, Monica realized what a nice night it had been. A Friday Fun Day that had actually been relaxing and rejuvenating, for her. It was so nice to talk to an adult, and share bits of daily life, without feeling as if it was a burden to them. Her ex had always made it feel like her life was a distraction from what was important, his life. It was pretty damn refreshing to just share, like equals. They even talked a little bit about work, the Mathewson Project and how Tim had done most of the work on developing the plan. It was amazingly easy to talk to him. It sounded like a great project, honestly. She still couldn't believe the cow had signed off on it. She wondered, briefly, how her note would go over, but it passed quickly as she watched her sons bowl.

Bowling went a little longer because Monica and Tim were so comfortable. They just kept adding games to the tally, letting the kids guide the night. When Billy began to get cranky, Tim realized they were edging into bedtime, and it was time to wrap this night up. Monica noticed the same thing and was impressed that Tim could read the signs. Oh man, her ex had really done a number on what she expected from men. He'd never been able to see a damn thing that had needed to be done. Tim was just a different species than her ex; it was that simple.

"Okay, guys, time to pack it in. I've got to get Leah and Ryan back home, and Billy needs to hit the hay." Tim gathered them up amidst the complaining and headed out. Monica and the boys did the same; they had a movie to watch still, when they got home. Late nights were still acceptable in these last days of summer.

While they fought over which action movie to watch, Monica poured a small glass of wine and thought about Tim and the kind of man he was proving to be. Seems like a grown-ass man, she laughed. No trace of the 'wrong-side of the track' type stuff from high school, and he was doing a great job of being a single dad. Not only could he handle his own life, but he also made her all sorts of horny. She sipped her wine and thought about Tim taking her on the sofa in her office. She wondered what he'd be like in a bed, with all the space that afforded. The yelling of the boys halted her reverie, and she left the wine to hang out with dinosaurs and geneticists.

CHAPTER 14

The weekend contained lots of Bears on patrols and phone calls with Harriet. She and her healers were completely confused by the found man-Wolf. He seemed harmless but wasn't receptive, at all, to any of the healing they were trying, and he was completely uncommunicative, just like the one they found last year. Max wasn't able to scent any new Wolf presence in town and the presumption was that they were gone. None of the pack was comfortable with that presumption, but there was no new information, and short of maintaining their patrols, there was not much to be done.

Tim sent Monica a short thank you text and that was it. He was determined to avoid all possibilities for venom, and figured the less communication, the less opportunity. It had been such a nice time, and he was thinking a lot about when he could see her again. He didn't really care about the venom. It was pretty harmless, really. She always had those sparkling eyes to fall back on. He wasn't sure she could control that part of herself. His Bear was constantly humming when it came to Monica. He could feel the bear within sharpening his claws. Tim wasn't entirely sure what to make of it.

On Monday, he made his way into the office after picking up his coffee at The Cup. Harriet had looked stressed, and Max was his normal quiet self.

The office was quiet, but Alice was on the phone in the back, with eyes closed and a grimace on her face, "Of course, of course. I'll check on it and get back to you." She hung up the phone. Tim gave her a questioning look. "Mrs. Mathewson has shown her true colors, Tim. I'm not sure the project is going ahead any longer. She's greatly concerned about the 'elements' the housing units could bring to the town. She got wind of the low-income portion of the project, somehow, and her inner 'disgusting person' is showing itself. But I'll be damned if she stops this project. You all have worked too hard. Hell, I've worked too hard."

Tim was rocked. He'd been working on this project for years. They'd had a breakthrough when Alice joined up with Mrs. Mathewson to forge ahead. He hadn't explicitly told Mrs. Mathewson that some of the homes would go to lesser-income people, but he hadn't really done it on purpose. Single parents? Working moms and dads who happened to have less income coming in? These weren't exactly vagrants moving into town! They were people who were already here, who'd suddenly be able to afford to own a home in town. It would give them a massive leg up for their families.

Bill walked in to see both Tim and Alice standing quietly in a state of shock. "What's up? What's happened?" he said.

After Alice explained, Bill started organizing their response. "This project is in the best interest of this town, and we all know it. Whom do we know on the Council who supports this? Ambrose, Monica, Jack, Who?"

Alice said, "Monica. She's evidently been on its side for all of its different permutations. Must benefit her brother some-how." She smirked unhappily.

Bill walked out of the office with phone in hand. "I'm taking care of this right now. Tim, be ready to schmooze. Brush your hair."

Tim looked at Alice with a questioning face. She laughed. "You're fine, Pops. No worries, your hair is just fine," she said.

Five minutes later, Bill returned. "Okay, Tim, you're going to Monica's office for a meeting, bring the portfolio presentation of the project, and get over there. You know where her office is, right? You guys mended whatever it was that was wrong, right? She made a weird noise when I told her I'd send you over."

Tim looked away from any eye contact. His Bear was basically roaring with the need to get over there. "Yeah, we're good. I'll go get ready. I know where it is. She's working with us, right? Not against us?"

"Yeah, yeah, she's with us. She's not a big fan of Mrs. Mathewson, but I know they've talked about the plans fairly recently, so I think she'll be of help in making sure Math-ewson is back on the team."

Tim headed to the back office to gather all the materials to prepare for the meeting. He was looking forward to getting back into Monica's office; he'd had really, really good luck there. His Bear growled his appreciation at the memory. He could feel himself blush as the thought entered his mind of her spread out on that sofa for him. Oh God, thank God his brothers didn't know he was a blusher. And damn, now he *was* going to have to act like nothing had happened, espe-cially if he wanted to get this project done. No sexy time for him, just work. He knew Monica would be all work, no play.

* * *

Monica got off the phone with Bill and was completely flustered. *Focus*, Monica, her inner voice yelled, yet again. Tim was coming over and last time he'd been here…. The memory of that sex was still banging around her brain. Even with the things that had happened this week, she didn't think she'd completely stopped vibrating. During bowling, with kids around, she'd been keenly aware of every ripple of muscle on him. She'd teased him about his tattoo, but really, had just wanted to see it again so she could remember his entire chest, and maybe put her face on it; just smell him. *Focus*!! Oh God, how was she going to *not* wind up on her back again? She freaking *wanted to*! Oh God, was she in trouble. She was definitely going to need to distract herself.

CHAPTER 15

Monica answered the office door after a flurry of whispered curses and a quick pat down of her hair. She'd been moving things and was a flipping mess. Great.

"Hi, Tim. I'm sorry for the mess, I was just moving the sofa around and got sidetracked, and so everything is just mid-stream. Please come in." Tim looked around the office. It seemed like Monica had moved every piece of furniture in the room.

"What's up? Rearranging? What for?" he asked, as he dropped his portfolio and briefcase on the sofa. "Want a hand?"

Monica put her hand on her hip and huffed. She was trying not to stare at him. She couldn't imagine that he knew how unbelievably handsome he was. Even in a button-down shirt and khakis, he looked like a sexy lumberjack. His arms bulged under the cotton, even while he looked totally professional. His hands were the perfect size for holding all her parts. He was so much bigger than she was, it was so easy to picture herself back in his arms. *Agh.*

The plan to re-arrange furniture to remove Tim from her memory was not going to work if Tim was all helpful and handsome and touching everything in the office. But having his help would make it take half the time. She definitely should not have started this project today, but she had found herself staring at the sofa and reliving sex, over and over.

"Okay, Tim, but just a little. I know we have actual work to do. I don't want to suck you into my designing fancy too far."

Tim smiled and did not say the innuendo-laden words that must have popped into his brain. Tim looked straight into Monica's eyes. She smiled too; she understood and appreciated his restraint. They spent a half hour moving furniture, and then, Monica called it to a close. "We've got to quit, or we'll never deal with the Mathewson thing. I could keep moving furniture for a week and not be satisfied. With what we've done, I'm going to need a new lamp and to change out the rug. Designers are notorious for redoing their spaces. Let's just leave it. I want to tackle Mrs. Mathewson now, if you're up for it."

"What happened with her, do you know why she's all up and bothered about it? We've been working on it for years; it's not changed lately… What got into her craw?"

Monica shrugged her shoulders. She wasn't going to tell him she'd sent a note pointing out the low-income element to that cow. She'd wanted her to *know*, not to cancel the whole thing. She was disappointed, but not surprised by Mrs. Mathewson. "No idea. We've got to present her with research and plans, all over again, so that she knows we're not building a tent city. Somehow, she thinks low-income means drug addiction and dissolution of humanity."

Tim sighed. "She was a *terrible* woman when I was a kid, talk about dissolution of humanity. I always felt so bad for her kids. I never had a good mom, but I still knew I was better off than they were."

"Huh?" Monica shook her head. "They had everything handed to them, and they were still hurtful losers. Your perspective is better than mine is, I'll admit. I'd just rather not deal with that kind of people."

They sat down and got to work, sitting on the floor around the coffee table because the sofa was now too far to be useful. Monica took her shoes off and curled her legs up under her. Tim watched appreciatively as she looked just like a sexy librarian, in her pencil skirt and her stocking feet. "You must have to deal with that kind of person all the time, though. Designer? Town Council? Talk about people who think something is owed to them..." Tim queried.

Monica nodded. "Yes, it can be overwhelming, at times. But the design work? I love it, so it doesn't matter so much that the people are obnoxious because they're letting me do something that I love and that I am good at. As for Council? That's not much fun. I took the job, originally, because someone was screwing my brother's chances at a successful business and the only way I could do anything was from the inside-out." She shook her finger at Tim. "I'm a slow, insidious invader, Tim. I always get my man."

Monica was just joking but realized, as it came out of her mouth, that she was pointing at a man that she may or may not be considering as a 'man man'. She quickly tucked her pointing finger under her legs and changed the subject. "What about you?" she asked. "Ursa Development has done really well for itself in what seems like, forever, but you all seem pretty low-key, nonetheless. How are you still the "Lawson boys from the wrong side of the track" when you've got all that success behind you?"

Tim had never had it put quite so boldly to him. He puckered his lips in thought. "Monica, you've just summed up the town's feelings about us, all in one sentence. I have to think." He looked at her like he was trying to think of what words could possibly answer all of that. "My mom left when I was six. I remember her, but it's really vague. My dad did the best he could, but it was rough, what with there being four of us under eight at the beginning. We always felt like we were the poor relations, even with our dad and uncles being so competent. The business changed hands a few times, and there was some drama with that. I guess, everything has always felt kind of up-in-the-air for me and my brothers, and we've all handled it in different ways. But, for sure, we got up to some trouble. In truth, it was no more than anyone else in their teen years, but it stuck with us, somehow. I think because we ran together as a pack. It was seen as some sort of definable personality trait. It's unsettling, really, to be identified by an action you took twenty or more years ago, in the midst of puberty and all sorts of changes."

Monica looked at him. "You're right, I still put you *all* in the same box you were in twenty years ago. It's strange. The rage I felt when you didn't recognize me came straight from my high school self. It had nothing at all to do with who I am now. I mean, it didn't help that I needed my coffee, but still, it was an echo of another time. Do you, even now, not remember me from school?"

Tim looked across the table at her. "Monnie, I honestly don't remember a lot of school. I know almost no one from that time, outside of my family, except for people I've worked with here in town. In school, I was barely able to look out for my brothers; I didn't have time for extracurriculars, and certainly, not girls. I didn't have many friends and I got through school by the grace of God and some exceptionally talented teachers. I escaped to college and that's when I started to finally be fully human. I started learning about women and then, was back in Mossy Ridge the week after graduation, marrying Terri. From then on, all my learning was about Terri, and almost none of it was good. Believe me, I would love to have known you in school. Imagine the stories I could have told in the locker room?" he laughed.

Monica laughed. It was so nice not to pretend with Tim. He wasn't acting as if they were strangers or holding it against her that she wasn't putting out every second of the day. He was treating her like a complete person. It was just so normal. It was nice, too, to talk freely about the past with another adult. She'd been married and never felt this comfortable with a man. *Hell's Bells. What the fuck did that mean?*

Tim watched as a series of emotions passed over Monica's expressive face. It was fascinating. She had heard people describe her face before. Anyone and everyone could literally watch her thinking happen. She'd started out sort of dewy-eyed and laughing, gotten bothered, then mad, then confused. He'd seen it before on her. He looked like he was trying to wait it out, not interrupt, and see what was coming. She'd had people watch her before, but it had a new weight this time and she really could *feel* him watching.

Monica could feel Tim's eyes on her, but this was too crazy, right? She was sitting on the floor in her office, with a man who she had fucked wildly on her sofa there. He'd just moved that sofa; he was like some kind of strong man in the circus, he probably hadn't even needed her there. His body was completely distracting. They were working and talking about the past, and it was just as natural as anything was, and supremely good. It was so good. She wanted him. She wanted him in a big way. She wanted him to come home with her at night. She wanted him in bed. She wanted him making coffee in bare feet in the morning. *What the fuck?* Monica was overwhelmed. She could feel her eyes welling up. She hung her head. "What the fuck." she whispered to herself.

Tim still watched. He probably heard her whisper. Monnie wasn't at all sure what was going on, but it felt like things had taken a turn for the worse. She'd gone back to dewy-eyed but now felt sad. *How could she want this guy this way?* Tim moved over to her side. "Monica? You okay? You just went from happy to mad to sad in the last few seconds. I love it when you're mad and sexed up but this one just keeps going. You want a tea or something?" He put his hands on her shoulders. "Want to talk about it?"

They were still sitting on the floor, like kids playing Legos. Monica looked up at him, looking concerned. She was in deep, deep trouble. She loved this guy, already. How could this possibly be? She'd known him since she was a kid, but he hadn't even known who she was before this week! Hadn't she learned anything from her ex? "Holy fuck," she said, her eyes wide.

Tim laughed. "Well, I think swearing is actually a good sign here. Anything I can do?" Monica interrupted him by getting up on her knees and knocking him right over onto his back with a kiss. They were completely tangled up in legs and limbs and Monica didn't care.

Tim was chuckling, almost nervously. He pulled back from the messy, delicious kiss. "Monica? Everything okay? You know we're on the floor in your office, during the full-office workday, right? And the door is open? And there *are* people here? This doesn't seem like you, as much as it is completely fucking cool with me. What is going on with you?"

CHAPTER 16

Tim was almost uncomfortable with the situation. Just scarcely. He just wanted to know if Monica was okay. He was not going to say no to her lying on top of him at any point, but he did want to be sure she wasn't having some sort of emotional seizure. She was continuing her lovely kisses and not answering any of his questions. He wanted her to want him, plain and simple, no hysteria at all.

Huh. That was interesting. Tim hadn't been entirely sure what he wanted. Having Monica laying on him, kissing him, was *definitely* something he wanted. His Bear was making all sorts of Mating sounds. And he already wanted more, more of the wild expression changes, more of the profanity. He wanted her stocking feet and he wanted her laughing at the bowling children. He was smack dab in love with this woman and it hit him like a ton of bricks. *Woah.* So much so that he lifted Monica off of him and set her on the ground. He sat up and looked at her.

"Woah, Monica. You know I love it when you attack-kiss but what is happening here?"

Monica untangled her legs and curled them back up

under herself. She looked very unsure right now but seemed to be struggling with what to say. She slid over next to Tim, right up close to his warm, good-smelling body.

"I am okay, Tim, I just … I realized a thing, and I have to say it right away or the moment will pass, and I don't want it to, okay? I'm not one to hide away once I know what I want to say and I don't want you to run off, okay? Just sit tight for a second."

Tim nodded, put his arm around her, and let her lean into his chest. It was so good to have her close. That she wanted to be there filled him with a lovely, settling peace. His Bear stretched out lazily. He felt like someone had just put a blanket over his shoulders. He sighed contentedly.

Monica looked up at him. "I want you, Tim. I want you in my life in a lot of ways. It's not just a sofa thing," she giggled and gave him a side-smile, "but I'd take more of that. I want your arms around me all the time. I don't know what I'm goddamn doing, but I want more of you." Monica stuttered to a stop.

Tim didn't trust himself to speak much. It was like a dream, someone just saying what they wanted, out loud, clearly. His Bear wanted nothing more than to claim her, claim her and make her his own. Tim tamped down cleanly on the impulse, cleared his throat and looked into her sparking green eyes. He moved his hands to hold her beautiful face and said in a deep, gravelly voice, "Yes, please" before leaning in to kiss her.

This was a new kiss. This was slow and deep and full of promises too delicate to speak. And it was, also, fucking hot. They started slowly but Tim's animal side wanted nothing more than sheer domination. Tim nibbled at her full bottom lip, he wanted to see it dragging along his cock. His breath caught. Monica cleared her throat. "Mmm, excuse me for a minute, Tim." She got up slowly, smoothing her skirt down her hips and walked out into the office suite, closing the door behind her. Tim could hear her speaking with the secretary but not the words spoken. He waited impatiently, still on the floor, still with a giant hard-on. *I am waiting for my mate,* he thought. This time the thought didn't upset him at all. This was what it was to know.

Monica returned, closed the door behind her, and walked to sit next to him on the floor. "If we wait about ten minutes, the office will be empty. I gave us all a half day, so I could work on the Mathewson Project exclusively," she smiled.

"Mmmm, I certainly do have a project for you," Tim teased, "but my cock has never been called Mathewson before. I'm not sure I can wait ten minutes for you to start work, Monica. I might have to get some papers together first." Tim reached over and undid the top button of Monica's blouse. "I'm going to get started on my research right here." His fingers drifted down into the blouse, following the rise of her breasts. "It seems, there are some obstacles to the project, here and here." Another button and he had both breast in his hands. At a flick of the nipple. Monica gasped. "What? Are you unhappy with my work on the project thus far, boss?"

Monica flashed a glance out the glass partition; the desk was empty and the light off. She sighed. "One more minute, Tim, let me lock the door, please." She got up and locked her door. She turned to him, smiling. "This project needs the utmost care and attention. The tiniest details need to be attended to, you see, in order for this to be a success."

Tim laughed outright. "Get your ass over here, Monica. We'll see about details. I'm a dedicated worker, I'll get you, I mean, *it* done right."

Monica sashayed over to Tim, still on the floor, laughing. He grabbed her hips and pulled himself up slowly, with his face pressing against her pussy, then belly and breasts. "I can already smell you, Mon. You started without me. I've got some work to do, just to catch up." He caught her lip in his teeth and tugged. Monica let out a little gasp.

"No more talking, Monica." He slid his hand up under her skirt, traveled over her ass to pull down stockings and panties, and dipped two fingers directly inside. Monica gasped again. "See?" said Tim. "Your pussy is already calling for me." He pulled his fingers out and put them in his mouth, slowly. Tim closed his eyes. The time for talking really was through.

Tim grabbed a throw pillow from the sofa and threw it on the ground. He pointed, and Monica lay down, fully clothed with her stockings and panties at her heels. Tim stood above her and disrobed. First, his shirt. As he pulled it over his head, Monica watched.

As the claw tattoo was slowly exposed, Monica's eyes got more clouded. She watched him and began arching slowly as she was getting more and more turned on. Tim began to undo his belt and reached in to adjust his cock. Monica couldn't stand the waiting any longer and crawled over to help. She unzipped his trousers and slid her fingers under the waist of his shorts, to slide them down and release his erect, bobbing cock.

Tim hummed. Monica grabbed the base of his cock and circled it firmly. With her other hand, she guided him into her mouth. Tim gasped. Monica moved his shaft back and forth into her mouth, licking especially around his tip, keeping one hand firmly at his base. Tim put his hands on her head, guiding her to take him deeper. Monica easily surrendered to his communication. She made a small humming noise and Tim shuddered.

Tim stepped back from Monica and looked at her with eyes clouded with lust. "You have too much clothing on, Monica. Let me help you with that." Tim knelt, his cock dripping with Monica's saliva and pre-cum. He pushed her down and slid her skirt, underwear and stockings off her in one quick motion. "You still ready for me, Mon?" He looked at her now half-dressed body with a barely concealed animal hunger. His eyes were darker than they'd ever been and Monica shivered and nodded. Tim stretched out along Monica's body, kissing her mouth while exploring her body with his hands. He did not skip dipping his hands into her body, and dragging his wet fingers up to her nipples, to spin and circle them.

Monica's blouse was open, her skin puckering and goose-pimpling everywhere. "You cold, Monica? You need some warmth?" Tim raised himself to lay on her completely, his groin pressed neatly against hers, his legs outside hers, and his forearms along her shoulders. "Warmer now? Can you feel me?"

Monica nodded, and shivered, but not from the cold. He was staring at her like he was going to eat her. She liked it. The way Tim had her legs pinned meant she had to lift her bum to get his cock to rest on her just right.

Tim slowly moved his cock against the lips of her pussy. "I want to go in, Monica. Can I go in?"

Tim asking her permission just liquefied her. On fire, she nodded and whispered, "Please."

Tim slid the tip of his cock inside her hot tunnel. His whole body shuddered. His arms shook as he tried to move slowly. She began to pull his body closer to her, to get him deeper.

Tim suddenly thrust fully. Monica gasped at the depth; feeling himself so far into her body brought such a satisfying pleasure. She arched in reaction and ran her nails down his back. Tim began fucking faster. "I can't hold back, Mon, I can't." He grunted. Monica smiled into his shoulder and raised her pelvis farther, allowing him full-depth thrusts. He was losing control, and she could feel it. She squeezed his cock inside her, over and over. Monica met each of his thrusts with one of her own, and the sweat rolled off his body onto hers. This was it; this was the best thing ever. Tim bucked and bucked, and his orgasm shot into her like fire. Monica arched back, taking him in as much as she could.

Tim collapsed on her, panting. After a minute, he whispered to her, "Oh my god, I couldn't hold on, Monica. Those squeezes killed me." He slid off to the side. "You're incredible. I can't believe I came that fast."

Monica just laughed. "I love that I can get you off that fast, Tim, and it leaves us time to *actually* work on Mathewson."

Tim raised up on his elbows. "Oh baby, just because I'm done, doesn't mean *we're* done. You are definitely due some attention, sweet thing."

Tim positioned himself between her legs, on his belly. "I'm in this for the long haul, Mon." Monica's head fell back as Tim began to lap at her soaking wet pussy, holding her thighs back with his hands.

Twenty minutes later, Monica could not have told you what her name was.

CHAPTER 17

They did actually make a plan about Mrs. Mathewson; they just did it while naked on the floor of the office. The plan was simple – kill her with kindness. They both knew this was not going to be a traditional approach with Mrs. Mathewson, but they were betting on the shock to her system allowing some new information into her hard cockroach-shell body. That approach, plus convincing her that the low-income homes would only be set aside for families, not indigents. The battle would be whether she cared at all about who was poor, or just that 'they' were poor.

"It's funny," Monica said. "I probably had less money growing up than you did, and a shittier family, and somehow, I was the 'upper-class' in high school, because of where I lived and how I looked. Mrs. Mathewson has no idea about who has the money in this town anymore, and we're going to spin that right into her hands. We're going to play her snotty ass like a fiddle."

Tim was a little chagrined at manipulation being their tactic. He didn't really like not being straight-forward about his needs. It didn't suit him naturally, but he could see that Mrs. Mathewson would need some careful consideration in order to get over her lifelong and disgusting biases. Tim was in charge of the kindness part; Monica absolutely refused. Tim was hoping maybe the perspective shift into hopeful possibility would be more helpful to them.

"What if we talk about the leg up that having these affordable houses will give to families, families who are already pulling themselves up by their own bootstraps, working, just 'starting out' as it were?"

Monica was dismissive. "Tim, you know this lady is a privileged, rich battleax. So do I. We don't have to play fair if she never has a day in her life."

Tim looked at Monica, laying naked next to him. He'd loved talking business on the floor of her office. He could not wait to get her into a real bed. His Bear stretched languidly as Tim's eyes roved over her body. *This was her; this was the one to claim.* Tim shook that thought out of his head. He was going to have to think about this thing with Mrs. Mathewson. Their meeting with her was for first thing the next morning.

"Babe, it's getting late, and I've got to get Billy from daycare. What time do you want to meet before we see her? I'll buy you a coffee at The Cup?"

Monica stretched; her breasts waved enticingly in Tim' s face.

Tim growled, "No fair, Monica." He bent over and licked each nipple. "I really do have to go pick up Billy."

Monica blushed and gasped as his tongue raised each nipple to a new peak. She pushed his head away; Tim reached over and pressed both her arms to the floor. "It'll just be a minute, Monica. I want you to remember me tonight." He bent his head to her breasts and nipped at her nipples until she was writhing beneath him.

Abruptly, Tim hopped up and grabbed his t-shirt, his cock bobbing, hard and erect again. "There you go, Monica. That's how I want you to feel until you see me again, like you can barely stand it."

Monica watched him get dressed from the ground, her mind almost melted with desire. Tim bent over and kissed her. "See you in the morning, beautiful."

Monica sighed and listened until the door clicked shut before she slid her hands down her body to her clit. Tim had absolutely brought her to the heights with just some nipple action; it was incredible. She was so wet for him, and so turned on; she'd barely even be able to walk out of here. This man was definitely different. She could barely believe her luck.

CHAPTER 18

The next morning arrived and Tim pulled open the door of The Cup. Monica was already there, sitting in the back, next to the community board. He was just so damn beautiful. She could see her nipples pushing against the silk blouse she was wearing, and she felt a pulse in her pussy at the sight of him. She had so many things she wanted him to do to her. He shook his shoulders like a wet dog, maybe he could feel her thoughts of him. Monica shook her head. He seemed excited this morning, like he had something to spill. She couldn't wait to hear when he told her what he was excited about. He came straight over, clearing his throat.

"Morning, gorgeous. Can I kiss you or are we being private still?" Monica looked up at him curiously.

"Hi, handsome, you look really nice today." She paused, "Yep, we're private till I tell my kids, okay? You ready to take down Mrs. Masterson?"

Tim pulled out a chair, his brawn making the chair look like a toy. "Yep, just wanted to check. Really would like to rumple you up, though." He looked her over appreciatively and sighed, sitting down. "Let me tell you, first, though, what I've got set up for today."

Monica raised her eyebrows. She really wasn't a fan of surprises or of someone adding events to her already full schedule.

"Mrs. Mathewson is going to meet us at the site in a half hour. I called her last night and changed the appointment. I want to show her and get her to dream with us about the walkability, the boost to downtown, and talk about giving her name something to be proud of."

Monica felt her face speaking her mind and tried to shut it down. Her head tipped to the side, "What about the plans we made yesterday? I thought we made them together! I'm not dressed for a traipse through the fucking woods, Tim!"

Tim looked down at her stiletto business-lady shoes and agreed. "I'm sure Alice has something you can borrow, Monica. Come on, this is a great idea."

Monica couldn't believe it; he'd completely thrown her under the bus. She knew how to work Mrs. Masterson. And now she was going to look like a fool in front of the old cow, which was the last thing she needed. She was no good at spontaneous situations, and she knew it. She was pissed at Tim. They'd had a plan, and she was going to excel at *that* plan. This was goddamned unreal.

She whispered her rage at him, spitting across the table, "I don't want Alice's fucking construction boots, Tim. I'm on the fucking Town Council. Imagine how unprofessional I'm going to look now! I don't want to fucking tromp in the mud with fucking Mathewson. She'd never let me hear the end of it. She's certainly not going in the woods with us. I'm not going to give her the satisfaction of seeing me dirty. She already thinks I'm a fucking tramp. She was a great friend of my father's, you know. You can do the damn meeting yourself, Tim, if it's so damn important to you to be in control of it. It's yours. Fucking welcome to it." She could feel the heat of rage emanating from him as she left. Monica grabbed her things and stalked out the door without looking back.

CHAPTER 19

Tim sighed and sat back at the table. It was a sigh of incredible fucking rage. Monica and her damn venom. It kept coming back. As much as he'd fallen for her, this did bother him. Who did she think she was? Why the hell would she be walking out on him about this? Shouldn't she have some filter when it came to him, making some attempt to be kind or attractive? Didn't she love him? Tim knew they hadn't been using those terms, but this was more than just a one-night stand. Well, he had thought so anyhow. Tim didn't know what was going on. He couldn't believe he'd been so suckered. He'd thought she was something special and she was just like every other crazy woman he'd ever known. His Bear moaned. He just had to get Monica's crap out of his mind and go meet Mrs. Mathewson. But it sucked that Monica had left him to do this on his own. He'd be really pissed if this deal fell through because he didn't have her by his side.

* * *

He got out of the Ursa Development truck a few minutes later, on the Mathewson land. His brothers had cleared a spot for him last night and he'd set up a table and chairs for the meeting. Monica would have been fine, whatever shoes she had on. She still thought he was a bumbling high school boy with no class, he guessed. He waited by the truck for Mrs. Mathewson. A large black town car pulled into the space created last night and the driver came around to let out a small but wiry old woman with a cane, a fierce demeanor, and a sharp eye. She did not look like a nice woman, but Tim had met many fierce people with hearts of gold, so he was suspending judgement, despite her reputation.

He walked up to Mrs. Mathewson with his hand out. She pointed to his truck. "Ursa Development? It used to be Ursa Lupine when I worked with them. What the hell happened? You lose a Wolf somewhere?" Her voice was unkind, bitter, and uncomfortable to listen to.

Tim cleared his throat. "I'm Tim Lawson, the Lupine part of the company changed hands before my time, Mrs. Mathewson. Would you please have a seat? I want to talk with you about this project. I have been working on it for several years, as I am sure you know. I can answer just about any questions you might have."

Mrs. Mathewson sat down, putting her cane on the table before her. "What I want to know is why I got an email from that Town Council floozy telling me about the indigents moving in, instead of one of my own people telling me about it! I do not give my permission for my land to be used for some sort of halfway house!"

Tim shook his head to try to make sense of the fifty wrong things that Mrs. Mathewson had just said. Monica was the floozy? She'd done what? Why hadn't she told him she'd been the one to start this trouble? What the hell was going on? Why did Mrs. Mathewson think low-income meant halfway house?

Tim sat down across from her at the table. "Mrs. Mathewson, no indigents are moving into this development, that, I guarantee. This is a neighborhood of small, family homes, within walking distance of our town center. I can't do more than guarantee you that with my word and the word of Ursa Development." He stopped and was done. There really wasn't anything left to say.

The silence grew. Mrs. Mathewson squinted her eyes at him and sighed. "You're just like all your family. So tough to deal with when there's no negotiation, just bald fact or aggression, just out on the table like this cane. I was looking forward to the hussy prancing all around me, trying to hustle me. Ones like her, I can eat for lunch." Mrs. Mathewson smiled. It was absolutely merciless, that smile, cold as ice.

Tim was growing to hate her, minute by minute. He needed to end this meeting before he decided to stop working with her entirely. He stayed silent another minute, and Mrs. Mathewson broke. She pulled her cane off the table and said, "Deal is still on. I'll be looking forward to dealing with Ursa Lupine again, or Ursa Development, as you call yourselves now." Her driver got out and walked her to her town car; she looked back at Tim as she got into the car and gave him a mock salute.

Tim had gotten up as she did and returned her gesture light-heartedly. He waited for her car to pull out and away before whooping and pumping his fist in the air. He looked around to be sure no one was there and sauntered over to his truck. He sat down to text Monica and realized he really didn't want to. He was really pissed that she hadn't been upfront about whatever note she had sent. What had she been trying to pull? Was she really that desperate for Mrs. Mathewson's approval? Was she really like that?

Tim texted Bill and Alice to tell them the news, and then, slowly pulled out.

He drove over to the daycare to get Billy. He felt like celebrating and he wished he wanted to see Monica, but he just didn't. He and Billy were the team that mattered at the very core, after all.

CHAPTER 20

*P*izza, video games, and a bouncy hut? Game on, as far as Billy was concerned. Tim chased him across the parking lot, just barely keeping him from certain death. Tim knew Frank was Monica's brother, but the connection between he and Frank was all about the pizza and Billy's love of the bounce, so it didn't cross his mind that there would be a problem. They paid, ordered their food, and Tim sat in front of an enormous pizza, watching his son bounce from game to game to game. It was Billy's heaven on Earth. Tim always felt like a million slightly over-stimulated bucks when he walked out of there, because Billy was so happy. It made all the stuff with Monica a little better. He couldn't get over the feeling of massive disappointment; somehow, he'd fallen for a woman who would turn on him, again.

Could he really have been that wrong? He'd definitely been swept up in something, and it had been just wonderful, and it had really made him think about his future in a different way. He'd daydreamed about Monica in his life going forward; was thinking about Luke and Brian being great friends for Billy to grow up with. Was he just a child, to be fantasizing like that? And, damn it, he'd just liked her. He liked her whole thing: the momming, the occasional venom, the body on her that never quit. Her emotions were crazy, but they were on the surface. You could watch her face to find out what she was feeling. And she was funny, the whole thing, the whole package. But that note to Mrs. Mathewson? And the way she walked out on their business meeting? He felt it deep down, an anger that he hadn't felt since Terri. The Bear was blessedly quiet.

Argh, he needed to change his mindset, maybe he just needed another pizza – pineapple, this time. He waved, and Frank walked over. "You okay, Tim? I've never seen you put away a whole pizza! Everything okay at work? Billy good?"

Tim sighed. "It's okay, Frank, just regular stuff. Got disappointed by a woman again. I think I might just stop trying; I mean, Terri did me in completely. I hadn't wanted to be hit by that again. I just felt really hopeful about this one. Like, it was a whole new kind of woman. She was a little scary, but I had already fallen for her when she shafted me. I'm just going to eat my pizza and look into monkhood."

Frank laughed. "Trust me, Tim, monkhood won't solve your problem. Not everyone has someone, honestly, but there's someone out there for you, I swear. Might even be this one. Take a breath. Watch Billy. Time works wonders. Don't look into monkhood, please. You'd be the worst monk in the world. Just eat your pizza and be happy." Frank put his hand on Tim's shoulder. "You're a cool cat, man. You'll be good."

Frank walked off, and Tim settled into his pizza and thought about Monica's breasts. He was definitely going to need another pizza.

onica got a text from Alice congratulating her for pulling off the Mathewson deal. She was sitting on the floor in her office, doing work on the coffee table again. She'd loved sitting on the floor with Tim. She was very glad that the deal was still on and more than curious about how Tim had pulled it off. She was both embarrassed and impressed that Alice clearly didn't know Tim had done it alone. He hadn't run and told Alice. It was definitely respectable. Or maybe she didn't mean anything to him, wasn't important enough to tell. If she could slump further down, she would. She'd been irrelevant, again. It was just as it had been with her ex. It was amazing, really, in the worst way.

He had never valued anything about her, not her love for her family, not her quirky personality, nothing. He'd hated her relationship with her brother. He'd hated her relationship with the boys because it had taken her attention away from him. Her time hadn't been valued; her opinions had been deprecated. She had felt the resurgence of that hurt and animosity when Tim ran over her plans without warning.

She couldn't believe she'd been so wrong about him. He'd just been after the conquest, hadn't cared for her at all. It hadn't even occurred to him to check in with her, as a partner would, an equal.

Men. Men and their whole mansplaining thing. He hadn't seen her plan as a way forward, but instead of saying so, like he would have to another man, he just blew it off, erasing her role entirely. He didn't have a shred of respect for her. How could she have been so stupid? She hadn't been able to keep her clothes on around him. But damn, *damn*. She had really liked him, really deeply. She'd really loved the casual way he was around her kids, the way he was with his own kid, the way he touched her and wanted her. Obviously, her instincts were completely wrong, again.

She didn't want to see him anymore. It hurt her a little to have that thought but he'd shafted her, and there wasn't any bigger red flag than that, and they'd just barely started whatever their thing was. As she thought about it, it began to hurt a little more, like a growing ache in her chest. She'd more than liked their time together. She'd said the 'L' word in her head. She'd been excited about him, ready to grow in a new direction with a new man. What was she going to do now? She wasn't going to find another man like that in Mossy Ridge. He was smart, handsome, and strong; there just weren't a lot of those to go around. *Whatever!* Monica was shouting at herself internally. She'd been decently content being single for a long time, she could get there again.

She had her boys, and her brother, and this town. She was going to be fine.

The ache in her chest grew.

im threw himself into his work. No woman was going to wreck him again. The Mathewson Development was going to change the landscape of Mossy Ridge, that's for sure, but in the most gracious of ways. The series of small, private homes were going to be attractive as well as practical. The neighborhood would back up onto the center part of town, providing more people and customers to a parched small-town economy. All the businesses in town were looking forward to it; the builders were chomping at the bit, and they'd had all sorts of interest in purchasing the homes, and they weren't even built yet.

There were also applications coming in for the low-income properties. Tim went through them personally, making sure there was nothing to satisfy Mrs. Mathewson's bias. He noticed that there were a few shifter families in the mix and was glad that the development would have a shifter presence to ensure a level of security. There were more shifters in Mossy Ridge than any of the humans were aware.

Tim realized he wasn't going to have to worry about

telling Monica anything about shifter life now. It was certainly a bittersweet realization.

He turned back to the work at hand. Monica was out of his life. It had just been a dalliance, nothing more. His Bear growled at the thought. It didn't entirely ring true to him, either, but he wasn't going to waste time on something that wasn't right. He'd lost enough time with Terri.

A phone rang in the office, and Tim turned to see Bill with a concerned look on his face. "Okay, we'll take care of it." Bill turned to Tim and Alice and said, "We need a repair crew at the Bouncy Hut. A car drove through the front door last night. We want to get him fixed up in time for tomorrow's last day of summer. Frank needs the business." Bill came over as Tim was getting up to make some phone calls. "Tim, the driver said he was trying to avoid a vagrant and his big dog, and they were both gone when he came to after the accident." Bill raised his eyebrows. "I'm not going to worry Alice about this, but I do want you to call Harriet and Max. Tell them to keep it on the down-low, okay?"

Tim was glad of the distraction, and made the calls to Harriet and Max, as well as gathering the materials to fix up Frank's entryway. He headed over to the Hut to get the right measurements and make the orders specific. If it looked like he thought, they might have the materials in-house, for some of it, which would make it easier. He pulled up to see Frank in front of the Bouncy Hut, looking defeated. Tim stepped out of the truck and walked over. He put his hand on Frank's shoulder and just stood and listened.

"They took the car out about a half hour ago," said Frank. "The driver wasn't drunk and was swearing up and down about a Wolf-dog and a vagrant. Some kids told me about a strange guy in the alley last week, but I looked and there wasn't anyone. I chalked it up to kid imagination." His voice cracked a little. "I really can't afford this, Tim! My insurance rates are already through the roof. I don't even want to claim it. This is my biggest week, the last days before school starts up. What am I going to do?"

Tim moved to look at him. "Frank, we got this. You take care of all of our kids at times; you're an important part of town. What do you need?"

As Frank came up with the list of what was going to need repairs, a giant golden Caddy roared into the lot. Monica climbed out, left the door open and ran to Frank. "Oh my *God*, Frank! Are you okay? Are you hurt? You said a car accident? What the hell? Why didn't you call me? Tim's here? My fucking car wouldn't fucking start, again, so I had to borrow Miss Crocker's! What's going on? Did the car go through the door?!" Monica was screeching, her hair was a disaster and her face looked like it had recently been pressed into a pillow, wrinkles, and all.

Frank went over to talk to her as she frantically brushed her hair with her fingers and tried to make herself presentable. It's possible she was still wearing a pajama shirt.

Tim turned, bemused, to wave, in the Ursa Development truck, carrying the materials to fix up the entrance. It would be a rush, but there was enough time for concrete to dry. It was nice to see Monica so clearly supporting and worried about her brother. No venom; just love in the form of worry. Too bad she didn't have any of that for him – just venom, and a willingness to walk out and leave him holding the bag. Too bad she only loved Frank.

Behind the incoming truck, at the edge of what was still-undeveloped land, Tim could pick out the shapes of two large animals. The hair on his neck prickled. His inner Bear knew, immediately, they were strangers, and they were a threat. Tim kept his eyes on them and pulled out his cell. He dialed Bill without a glance and whispered, "Bill, two Wolves at Mathewson. North of the parcel. Two shifters here besides me and two townies, Frank and Monnie. I definitely want more presence here. Get Harriet and Max here now." He hung up without another word and took a protective stance at the edge of the area.

The other two workers in the Ursa truck were looking at him intently. They must have smelled the change in demeanor. The air was rippling with the tension coming off him. He waved them over and talked with them about the situation in a very low voice. They were to continue on as if there were no threat but were to keep Monica and Frank in sight at all times, and when backup arrived, one man would take them inside, away from any action.

The Wolves hadn't moved. Tim couldn't tell if they didn't know they'd been spotted or if they were waiting for something. Either choice had consequences. If those Wolves couldn't tell they'd been spotted, then something was wrong with them. If they were waiting, what on Earth were they waiting for?

Harriet and Max rolled in, Max already in Wolf form. She drove around behind the Bouncy Hut, out of sight of the Wolves. Max loped to the front and was immediately nose to the ground. Harriet walked over to say hello to Monica and Frank, and then strode, more purposefully, over to Tim. "We were already on our way because of the 'vagrant and dog' story, Tim. I just told Monica and Frank that Max is my dog. I'm not sure he looks like anyone's dog, honestly. We'll deal with that later. We got Bill's call seconds ago. I can see them there. Not very well hidden, are they?" Harriet brushed her hair from her face. "It's almost like they are waiting for us, or someone. I wonder who it is. All the other man-Wolves we've caught are too messed up to be involved in this. And they were messed up before we came on the scene, I think. Let's get a few more shifters here, and then, we'll send out a team, see if they'll just tell us what they want."

Monica called out, "Tim?" as more Ursa trucks rolled in. Backup had arrived, and one of the guys was gesturing to the building where Monica and Frank were standing. Monica was looking concerned and gestured to Tim. Tim turned to Harriet, "I'll be right back. Yell if you need me."

He jogged over to Monica, "Hi, Monica, What's up? Everything look okay?"

Monica squinted her eyes at him. "What's happening over there, Tim? Why does it feel like SWAT is arriving here? Does this have anything to do with Frank or what happened to the Hut?"

Leave it to Monica to cut right through the niceties. Tim sighed; a little truth wouldn't hurt here and would stay little. "Monica, there's some people in the woods and I called my family to be here in case it was dangerous." He turned to Frank. "Remember that vagrant, Frank?" He tipped his head back to Monica. "I want to make sure you and Frank are safe and that there is no more damage to the property. It's work, Monica. This is what I do, you know, protect people."

There was a lot more he felt himself wanting to say, about how he would never abandon *her*, never leave *her* in the lurch, but it was all too much. If she was in danger, it erased some of his feelings of betrayal. It was just more important for her to be safe. He needed her to be safe. His hackles were up. He could feel the tension of the Bears around him, and knew it was time for her and Frank to go inside. "Just go inside until we sort it out, Monica, please."

Monica glared at him, and he glared back. He wanted, so badly, to bite her at the back of the neck and drag her inside to safety. Really badly, his Bear wanted to rise to the surface and carry her off. He was literally struggling to keep his Bear under control. That had never happened before. But, finally, she grabbed Frank's arm and steered him into the Bouncy

Hut. The one shifter left to go in with them looked pleadingly at Tim.

"Sorry, dude, you pulled the short straw," said Tim. "Don't let them come out until I give you the all-clear, okay?" The man nodded and Tim went back out to see Max making his way slowly into the woods. "What'd you decide?" he asked Harriet.

"Max says their posture is particularly non-threatening, almost like an elder's, so he's going in submissively to see if they're going to communicate. We're watching for any sign at all of aggression, and then, it's full-speed intervention."

Tim looked over at Bill, who was staring into the woods fixedly. "What do you think, Bill?"

Bill shook his head. "Honestly, I have no idea, but I'm having a hard time keeping my Bear from roaring out and ripping their chests open. The buildup of weird things this couple of weeks is really weakening my resolve."

Tim nodded. "I get it. Knowing Monica and Frank were here freaked me right out. Me? I can handle anything. Two delicate innocents? No way, I needed the full brutal force of Ursa. I felt like biting Monica, just to subdue her and make her go inside just a minute ago."

Bill spit out a laugh. "Kid. Biting a woman doesn't subdue her. It marks her as your mate. How can you not know that? You have real feelings for Monica?"

Tim snorted. "Monica? Are you kidding? There's only so much venom a man can take."

Bill still stared into the woods. "Marking a woman is a big deal, Tim, if your Bear wanted you to, you should really look at that." Tim looked down.

The forms in the woods began to move toward them, and all the men were immediately on alert. Max led the way to Tim and the others, shifting from his Wolf form as he got closer. One of the men handed him some sweatpants and he stood bare-chested by Tim and Bill looking down at the two Wolves sitting nearby.

"I have no idea what to tell you all, but there is something really wrong going on in the pack I escaped from. These aren't elderly Wolves, they're almost infantile. I don't know how they made it all the way down here without being killed. Between the woods and the roads, they're hardly competent to travel, and they are certainly no danger to Mossy Ridge."

Bill called the team to stand down, looked at Harriet, and she nodded. She and Max got the Wolves in the car and took off to the Tribunal. Tim turned to the Hut to see Monica standing by the side of the building; she looked like she was holding onto the wall. Her hands were spread out wide, and she was breathing deeply. He could hear that she was talking to herself, saying, "You are okay, you are okay."

He walked over, "Monica? You okay? Why are you outside? Where's Frank?"

Monica put out a hand to Tim's chest. "Tim. Tim, I just saw the most fucked up thing I have ever seen in my life. I don't know how to fucking process it. I must've done a drug, somehow, or maybe I inhaled concrete dust or something. Asbestos, maybe there is asbestos in the Hut. Tim, I just saw a man and a Wolf be the same thing. Like, it was a Wolf, just trotting along, and then, it shimmered and stretched and boom, it was Max. *Max*! And naked! And just Max. He put pants on, and everyone talked to him like it was no big thing. No big thing! What the fucking fuck, Tim?!" Monica was fully yelling, plenty of heads were turning, and heads were shaking, and occasionally smiling. It was the most common reaction of all, and each shifter could remember at least one like it.

"Monica," Tim said, "Listen, I know it's crazy. It's totally insane, I know. But it's Max, remember. You like Max. You trust Max. If there is something amazing and magical about

Max, it doesn't change that you like and trust him, does it?" He couldn't help thinking that he could be talking about himself.

Monica yelled, *"He changed into a man, from a Wolf!"*

"I know, Monica, I know. Take a breath, please. Remember Max. You like him and you trust him. Just like you used to like and trust me."

"Fuck you, Tim; this isn't about trust! It's about the whole world exploding. A person just changed into an animal! I just saw a fucking man-Wolf and not one single person has told me I'm crazy. This isn't about you. I need to get Frank and get the hell out of here. I must be having a stroke. I don't care if you saw it too; I'm clearly out of my mind."

Tim let her go. He turned to Bill and the guys, and just shrugged his shoulders. He got some jeers and some laughs and a few serious looks. Sometimes, it was a long and painful process when someone learned about shifters. It didn't always end well, and human-shifter relationships were a challenge. Bill walked over and put his hand on Tim's shoulder. "Well, it's a beginning, Tim. Now, she knows that shifters exist. Next, you tell her you are one. It won't be as hard now."

Tim scoffed, "Tell her? Why? So she can swear and yell at me next? What are you talking about, Bill? She didn't handle that at all! She's known Max for years and can't get over it. I have no intention of telling her, and why the hell would I tell her, anyhow? She does not need to know anything else about it, ever. Let her think she stumbled upon a bad mushroom; I don't care."

Bill laughed right in Tim's flustered face. "Oh my god, Tim. Give her a few minutes to adjust to her world exploding. Your Bear knows what's what, even if you don't. Go home, Tim. We've got this covered."

Tim checked that Frank's place would be done in time for

tomorrow and then, he left the site, shifting as he thought. There were no more civilians around. Frank had gone home with Monica, he presumed. He needed some time to unwind and think, and evidently, to check in with his Bear. Why the bite? He'd never had the impulse to bite anyone before. He wanted to sink his teeth into her and mark her, forever, as his. Why? He plodded off into the woods, where he and his Bear did their best thinking.

CHAPTER 23

*B*ut, of course, Frank hadn't gone home with Monica. He'd begged Monica to leave him to clean up his precious Hut. He'd watched the whole exchange between Monica and Tim, and then between Tim and Bill. He was standing at the former entrance, with a broom in his hand, looking stunned. He watched Tim the Bear trundle off into the woods. And, before that, he had heard Monnie yelling about Max and a Wolf. Frank's eyes were saucer-like. He continued staring into the woods for a long time, even as workmen began rebuilding his storefront all around him. The shifter who'd watched them earlier was on the phone to Bill, keeping his eyes on Frank the entire time.

The next morning, though, unbelievably, Frank opened on time. The entryway definitely looked freshly repaired, but it would function perfectly for the last day of summer vacation. And it looked to be a rainy one too, so it would help Frank with all his monthly costs. Tim and Ursa had done all of it and they hadn't even submitted a bill. Well, not yet at least, but it didn't sound like they would, the way Tim had been talking. Tim had come by to check on Frank, before the opening. They'd walked outside, strolling the parking lot.

"Frank, I know what you saw yesterday. Do you have any questions? Is there anything I can help you with?"

Frank looked stunned, again. "I, uh, thought it was a big secret, Tim. I didn't think we'd be able to talk about it or maybe someone would 'get me' if I saw it or something…"

Tim laughed. "Its not the mafia, Frank. I'm still the guy who eats pizza when confused, my kid is a monster in a bouncy house. Mossy Ridge is flat-out full of shifters, Frank. It has been for ages. We just keep a low profile, to keep people feeling safe. I'm glad you know, actually; it is hard to keep secrets from friends."

Frank laughed. "You have eaten a lot of pizza since you met Monnie, Tim." He looked at the ground. "You gonna tell her, Tim? She really has a lot of trust problems with men. I mean, this is a pretty big deal. I mean, it is for me, and I'm just friends with you, not like 'loving' you, you know?"

Tim looked over at him. "Monica isn't loving me, Frank. She is full of venom and spit and I don't know, let's just say she is not a fan."

Frank laughed and put his hand on Tim's shoulder. "Look, Tim, Mon is a handful, but she is worth it. All that vinegar is just to protect her sweet insides. She's the most loving person I know. You gotta tell her, she can handle it, I swear, just do it slow. You want me to help?"

"No, Frank. I'm not even sure I want to know her anymore. She really shafted me. Seeing her reaction to Max leaves a pretty sour taste in my mouth. I just wanted to be sure you would be okay, that you weren't scared or anything."

Frank dropped his hand off Tim's shoulder and took a deep breath. "I am freaked out, not gonna lie, Tim. But I can tell I'm going to get over it. It's the same people I've known for years, I mean, I *know* you, bear or not. Keep your mind open, too, Tim, about Monica. There's a lot more in there than spit and venom."

Tim nodded. Frank walked back into the Hut and Tim drove off to get little Billy,

* * *

AT LUNCH, THE BOYS SETTLED INTO THEIR BOUNCE-ARCADE-bounce routine, and Frank and Monica sat behind the counter, eating sandwiches. Monica was less disheveled but seemed to still be in a state of shock. She just sat quietly and let Frank get their drinks and their food. It wasn't like her at all. She just felt stunned. Frank put down his drink and took her hand. "Monica, I've got something I really need to talk to you about, and you are *not* going to like it."

Monica took her sandwich back out of her mouth and put it down. She looked at him silently.

More shocks, what's this one going to be? Monica wondered and sighed. Frank sighed too. "Monica, there are people in this town that change into animals, and vice versa." He sat back.

She raised her eyebrows. "I know. I mean, I saw Max, yesterday. You mean there's more like him, here, in Mossy Ridge?"

Frank spoke slowly, seeming to continue his own processing. "Seems so, I think it's something that may have been in Mossy Ridge for a long time. If you think back, there's always been, like, animal issues here, you know? We've had packs of creatures at times, and it's just not that normal in this state, but it is here, for some reason. I think there might even be families of shifters. That's what it's called, you know, shifters. I Googled it last night. Most of what I found was way too weird to be true, but the people who are both animal and human? Shifters."

Monica looked at him. "Why the fuck are you so calm about this, Frank?" Frank laughed; at least she was coming out of her shock a little. She was getting ticked off at Frank. *What the hell.*

"Well, I mean, I can hide from a lot of things, but not what I see with my own eyes. I mean, how can I argue that it doesn't exist if I witnessed a man turn into a Bear in front of my eyes? I'm not that dedicated to my old belief, I guess. I mean, there *are* clearly people who can turn into animals. And they are not dangerous to me, that much I believe too."

Monica scoffed. "A Bear. You saw a Bear? It's not just Max? Could Max be any animal he wants? For fuck's sake. I'm glad you are so laid-back, Frank. I'm not sure I don't want to call Homeland Security or something. Maybe the FBI? I mean, what are we dealing with here?"

"Monica, this is Mossy Ridge. Max, for one, is a good guy, who is our friend. Are you so scared of Max that you would destroy his life?"

Monica rolled her eyes. "I'm not scared, Frank. I'm just trying to do what's right for Mossy Ridge."

"Mossy Ridge? You think calling in Feds on people who live in Mossy Ridge that you don't happen to understand, is good for Mossy Ridge? What are you so scared of Monica? Nobody has threatened us, me, you, the kids, nothing! There is literally no threat here. This isn't like Dad."

As soon as it was out of his mouth, Frank's eyes went big. Monica turned to him with her own eyes wide. "What the fuck are you talking about, Frank?" The heat was radiating from her body. She felt like she was going to fucking explode. Monica's eyes were moving frantically, the only outside 'tell' that she was thinking a series of complex items.

She took a couple of deep breaths before saying, "I'm

completely floored, Frank. I don't understand you at all. You are telling me that I'm supposed to be okay with animals – shifters, I mean. Is that what I am hearing you say?"

Frank nodded.

"Because… I'm afraid of …. something like Dad?" Monica's voice cracked a little and got quieter as she asked what was really on her mind. "Dad? What are you talking about? Frank, what is going on here?"

Monica closed her eyes. She could feel her shoulders fall as she looked at him. He knew her best in all the world. She had to at least think about what he was saying.

Frank took a deep breath and kept his hands on Monica's hands. She was sure he was trying to keep her from bolting. "Dad was no good, Mon. We both know that. But even as a Wolf, Max is better than that. He's better than Dad. I feel like you think everyone is like Dad, dangerous and a liar. I just want you to stop it. Dad's gone. He can't hurt us anymore. Your stupid ex is gone. *Max* isn't a danger to anyone. You *know* him. You've got to just calm down. There are lots more good, honest men out there, more than just me even, although I am clearly the best of the best.' Frank snorted. Monica snorted too. She looked up at him and removed her hands from his.

"I'm not going to tell you I'm calm and cool like you, Frank, but I do see your point about Max. I need to chill out. I'm not calling the fucking feds. As for Dad? I've got some more thinking to do on that one. There is a small part of me that knows he did the best he could. It's a tiny, tiny part. And I can't really believe you're this calm about this. I can't. All I can do is try, right Frank? I'll try."

Frank stayed quiet. Monica needed the time. She knew he knew. It was amazing having a brother like this. He was her rock. She'd thought maybe Tim could be too, but that had gone to shit. Frank looked around at the kids in his Bouncy Hut, having the best time of their days.

"Monica, look. I mean, really look." He waved around. "This is Mossy Ridge; this is what you've been working for all this time. A safe place for kids to be kids. So, something doesn't fit what we've 'always known'. Look at the Lawsons, Tim, they made this possible. They fixed the Hut, basically, overnight, to give the kids a place to be kids. They had the worst reputation in school, but they are not scary bad guys. Tim especially, Monica. Whatever happened between you two, you can work it out. He's a good, decent man, Monica. You deserve someone like him."

Monica whispered, "He's a problem, Frank."

Frank laughed. "I bet, Monica. I bet." Frank left Monica to go tend to the Skeet Ball machine. Someone had managed to get a baby bottle stuck in the 200-point tunnel. Monica watched him work his magic with the kids he passed. He probably needed some time to process all this himself, no matter how calm he seemed. Her thoughts kept coming back to shifters. *What about the kids? Are the kids little Bears? little wolves?*

onica looked around at all the yelling, happy kids. The parents were relaxed and watching their kids from the edges of the action. It was a great family place in town. She was so glad it was open today. She turned to look at the repaired front doors and marveled at the work that had been done. She was so happy for Frank that this hadn't been another disappointment in his life. He'd make it through the slow season because of this one, super-busy day. The rain was the cherry on top.

While she was looking at the front doors, Alice walked in behind Leah and Ryan, her two rambunctious kids. Monica couldn't help but study them for signs of 'shifter'ness. If Max was something, anyone could be.

Alice walked up smiling, "Monica? What are you doing behind the counter? You helping out today? Leah and Ryan were dying to come over here today. Evidently, this is a big pre-teen hangout now. Your boys here?" Monica was staring at her intently, and Alice tapered off. "Everything okay, Monica? You feeling okay?"

Monica nodded. Frank walked over then and gave Alice a

kiss on the cheek. "We had a ruckus yesterday, Alice. Bill and Tim and the boys were all here fixing up the place. You've got to thank them for me, from us, all of us."

Alice gasped. "That was here? Bill told me some of it, but not where it was going down." Alice looked wildly at the two of them. "Oh my god, Monica? Was it you? Um, did you see anything really strange last night, improbable even? I heard there were drugs maybe?"

Monica squinted her eyes at Alice. "What do you mean, Alice? Do you think I'm suddenly doing drugs, or do you mean that there are people who turn into animals in Mossy Ridge? And they are called shifters and maybe you *are one*?"

Alice's eyes got wide. And then, she laughed. "Oh God, I wish I were, Monica! Can you imagine what it would do to child behavior if we could suddenly look how we feel? God, I would love to scare the hell out of them, every day, right around 9 o'clock." Alice sighed. "No, Monica, I am just a plain old woman. I can't be anything more than a tyrant some-times. Come sit with me. I do know an awful lot more, now, than I did when I found out."

Monica looked at Frank, and he gestured that she go.

Alice led Monica over to one of the tables, far away from the screams of the bouncy house area. "Monica, Bill is one. He's a Bear. What do you want to know? Ask me."

Monica sighed. "What the hell, Alice?! How can you be so nonchalant about this? I mean, he's your partner! How did you get to be okay with it? You let him near your kids?"

Alice gave her a look. "Monica, are you questioning my mothering? You seriously think I would let my kids be around a dangerous man? My mom might have done that, but I would not. Bill is the most amazing man I have ever known. And he is a man, Monica, not an animal. Shifters have an amazing magic to them. Watching Bill shift and knowing that Bill is still in this enormous Bear, is absolutely magical. It is pretty fucking hot, actually. He's, by far, the strongest man I know. He's my champion, and my soul is at rest knowing that he is keeping my kids and my heart completely safe, all the time."

Alice sighed. "Look, Monica, this is one of those times where you just have to accept it, even if it's hard. Mossy Ridge is full of shifters, and yeah, you didn't know. It wasn't some specific conspiracy to keep Monica in the dark; it's how it's always been here. There have been shifters guarding us our whole lives, and none of us know about it. It's a pretty thankless task, frankly, but they just keep doing it. Do you have anything you actually want to know or are you just determined to be freaked out and mad? You going to move on from that or just stay stuck in it?"

Monica looked at Alice, with weary eyes. "I'm just so tired, Alice. I'm doing the best I can, I really am."

Alice looked at her friend more keenly. "Okay, Monica. What do you want to know? Is there anything else going on besides the whole shifter thing?"

"Oh God, Alice. How can there be anything else?" Monica put her head in her hands. "How can I be thinking of Tim and his freaking shoulders at a time like this? Why do I want to call him and ask him to cuddle me tonight? I just want him to freaking cuddle me, with his giant goddamned biceps all in my face. I cannot believe my own brain! What is happening to me? There are freaking shifters in the world and I'm a freaking thirteen-year-old girl again. I KNOW better than to get involved with another guy like that."

Alice's eyes were wide. "Like what? Why are you, you're stuck on Tim?! Are you and Tim a thing? When did this happen?"

Monica sighed. "No, we're not. I thought we were, but I was wrong. I thought it was really something, but he did what all men do. It had nothing to do with this whole shifter business. It had to do with the Mathewson deal. I had a plan, and he threw it out the window. I didn't mean anything to him, certainly not my *brain*. I walked out, and he did his plan anyhow. It worked, thank god, but it was what broke us."

Alice squinted her eyes at Monica. "You walked out? Tim did that whole deal by himself? Monica! You know how much that deal means to this town! You just walked *out*? On Tim? The man who has already been walked out on one too many times! I didn't know you were such a bitch, Mon. I mean, I love you, but holy shit. You actually walked out on work, a man, and the town, all at once."

Ugh. That was brutal. Girlfriends were supposed to back you up against the guys. But Monica hadn't thought of the Terri part of Tim's past at all. She'd only been hurt that he'd planned something without her.

"Oh my god," she whispered as she sighed. "It's just too much. I'm the jerk again, aren't I? It's my fault, isn't it? What the hell? What do I do with this?"

Alice looked at her again. "Well, you might have to wait and see what *he* does, honestly. What do you *want* to do with this, presuming you get another chance to do anything?"

Monica looked down at her hands. "Right now, I have no idea. I think I need to go take a bath, Alice. Will you tell Frank I'll be back for the kids this afternoon?"

Alice nodded and gave her a hug. Monica gathered her things and waved at her boys. She made her way home in something of a fog, and made the hottest, most perfumed, bath she'd ever had, and sat herself down to soak.

Alice was right. She'd been completely unprofessional and jeopardized a project that had been years in the making because she didn't like the way Tim did it, or that it took her out of the spotlight. It had hurt, a lot, that he hadn't consulted her. It had been a huge blow to her confidence in him. She'd gone home that day and spent hours going over the experience, and she'd been completely overwhelmed with self-loathing. It had almost felt like mourning, like something in her had died again. She couldn't stop thinking about how little anyone loved her.

She never even knew what the new plan was; she just ran because her ego was bruised and battered. And instead of handling her pain like she always did, with a calm and professional demeanor, she up and walked out on the man she loved. What the fuck? Wait. *She loved Tim?* There wasn't any part of her that doubted that, and Monica was very surprised at the realization happening to her. She'd said it to herself before but was just as surprised the second time around.

But she would, for sure, have to figure out why she'd been so quick to show him the backside of her. Why had it been so upsetting to have the plan changed? Why was the pain so immediate and visceral? What was her problem?

Monica soaked, and thought, and remembered. And stumbled on what would have taken a year and six thousand dollars to a good therapist to find. She sat straight up in the bath and said, "Oh my good god."

She got out of the bath and began to get dressed.

onica walked back into the Bouncy Hut. She was feeling more in control, which was good, because Frank told her Tim and Billy had arrived just a few minutes prior. She didn't know if she should be on high alert or if they should all just sit back and watch the fur fly, as it were. It was a damn shame Alice had just left.

Monica walked up to Frank. "I'm good, Frank. That bath did me wonders. Boys okay?"

"Of course, they are," said Frank. "I'm not sure they completely registered that you left. They've been on the fruit slicing game for ages. Well, Brian has. I think Luke might be trying to flirt with that little girl in the blue shirt."

Monica was surprised and looked over to see Luke leaning against a game, watching a little girl play. It was a little bit awesome to see him smiling and looking shy all at once. "Man, things change so quickly around here, Frank." she said.

"Tell me about it," said Frank carefully. "Um, I need you to be chill with Tim, Monica, no shouting about shifters in here. I owe Tim tons for the fact that I am even open today, and I won't have you assaulting him in any way."

Monica stepped back. It was very rare that Frank stood up for himself. It was definitely worth noting. "I swear, Frank, I won't do a thing. We both owe him. I'll behave," she paused, "Thanks for warning me he's here though. I needed the warning."

Monica turned to find herself looking directly into Tim's chest. "You need a warning that I'm here, Monica? What do you think I'm going to do exactly?"

Frank's eyes were bulging out of his face. Monica put her hand on her brother's arm to reassure him. "Woah, Tim, I just needed the warning because I've got to apologize to you, and I was looking for some time to get my thoughts together."

Frank let out an enormous sigh.

"Frank, go do what you need to do, I'm done freaking out for a little bit, okay?"

Frank walked off into the arcade, looking behind him as he went.

Monica turned back to Tim. "Frank just warned me not to assault you in public, Tim. I can definitely promise not to do that, okay? I owe you a big apology for my behavior."

Tim scoffed, "For what, Monica, for freaking out about Max? For calling him an animal? For your utter disgust at a longtime friend?"

Monica cleared her throat. "No, actually, it may not have been pretty, but I think my reaction to being shocked out of my whole world view was pretty spot on. I may feel differently now, but I can't apologize for what I did yesterday. I've got to apologize for something else entirely."

Tim shook his head, "I'm not sure I can hear it today, Monica—"

"Just try," Monica interrupted. "I have to tell you about

my ex, and you just have to sit for it, because you have to. Come, sit down here."

Tim sat.

"When we were married, I knew he wasn't that good at being a husband, but I didn't really care. I assumed that what I felt was love because we were married. Really, that's all it took for me. But he was never the same way, and it took me the whole marriage to realize it. The last straw was a plan we had made, to go away for a weekend, to a fancy place on the coast. I'd gotten dressed to the nines and was waiting at the house for him to get home from work. The kids were at my cousin's house, and I was very excited. He walked into the house dressed to go for a hike. I mean, the full nines. His full nines. He was wearing a backpack and had binoculars. It was like a costume almost. He'd changed the plans totally, to involve tent camping at the nearby state park. When I objected, and pointed to my shoes and my overnight bag? He screamed that I never wanted to do anything fun, and that he was going anyway. I spent the weekend with the boys, alone, and learned later, he'd taken the woman he now wants to marry.

"I felt so hurt by you, but it was way beyond what might have been rational upset. I can't really excuse my behavior with you this week, my reaction was a little bit out of my control, but it had everything to do with me, and little to do with you. I'm so glad you went ahead and sealed the deal and that my past didn't uproot a project that has been years in the making. I would have been devastated to ruin that. I am just really sorry for it, all of it."

* * *

TIM HAD BEEN WATCHING MONICA WHILE SHE TOLD HER story. It was obviously something upsetting to her, and her sincerity was plain. He just didn't know if it fixed anything in terms of how he was feeling. He understood she hadn't abandoned him on the project; well, she had, but it had been almost a PTSD reaction to her own past. Part of *his* upset at the betrayal had been ancient history as well, so he recognized the truth of what she was saying. He could apply the same emotional logic to his response – feeling emotionally abandoned wasn't really a workplace commonality, after all. But her reaction about Max? That cut to the quick, wounded him and his whole family, and he couldn't move on from that, no matter how normal she thought it was.

"I hear you, Monica, I do. And I accept your apology about the Mathewson thing. I can even understand it, as I've got my own past to deal with. But I don't want to be friends, or anything else. I can work with you, and be cordial, but I think it's better if we just cut our losses."

Tim knew it was a little harsh but thought, sincerely, that it was for the best. The look of hurt on Monica's face, just a flash, was hard to see though, and knowing he was responsible for any more hurt to her, gave him a surge of guilt.

* * *

MONICA WAS HURT, BUT JUST FOR A FLASH, AND KNEW HE WAS more than justified in saying those things, not that she had been asking to start up again. There had been a small part of her that had been hoping he'd sweep her up in a passion of forgiveness. But she had literally walked out on him. It wasn't any misunderstanding. It was a shame to let it go, but she was not going to wait and seek and hope for another man, ever again. What he was saying did not leave much possibility for hope.

"Okay, Tim, I understand. I just wanted you to know how sorry I am, and how little it had to do with you. I am still working on things; I guess, more than I knew. I will see you around town. Give Billy a kiss for me."

Monica walked back behind the counter to where Frank was, shook her head at his concerned look, and continued into the back room, where she could have a minute of privacy.

TIM WALKED OUT TO WHERE BILLY WAS TRYING TO WHACK A mole and bent over to help, his face a mask of concern and thoughtfulness.

Frank watched them both and shook his head.

CHAPTER 26

Sitting in the break room, Monica's shoulders shook with the force of her tears. She knew she was disappointed but had been surprised when the tears came. Tim was a lovely man, and she had blown it, like she blew it every time. The shifter stuff hadn't even mattered, when it came down to it.

It was all about Tim. He was great with her kids, he was a hard worker, and he was hot as hell. Maybe it was the shifter in him that made him so strong, so big… What the hell was her problem? Why would she have flashed back so hard? It was past time to blame her ex for all of her issues; she couldn't drag him with her into every new relationship she had. Her sobs slowed, and she got herself gathered back together. Her kids were out there, and she needed them to see her looking okay, not emotional. They'd seen enough of that already this week.

* * *

Tim was just pretending to help Billy with the whacking game. Billy didn't need any help hitting things. If anything, Tim should probably redirect him before his aim got better. Monica had looked so sad, really, the whole time, retelling a story of her marriage, apologizing. If he ever got his hands on that dick, he'd show him a thing or two about how to be a man and a partner.

Tim was surprised by the vehemence he felt about Monica's ex. He'd just 'cut his losses' and what did it matter now? He kissed Billy on the head and recalled that Monica had asked him to. She was a good woman, a great mom, and she was devoted to her family. She didn't deserve a loser who rode over her just to throw her away.

And then, it occurred to him that he really had done the same thing. He didn't wear a costume and break a vow, but he hadn't shared his plan, he hadn't given her any warning of his desire to take a different approach, at all. He'd completely ridden over her. She'd reacted strongly but so had he, and it was all to do with Terri, really, not Monica. A natural upset had mutated into a really personal, historical *Deja vu*. He had hurt her, too.

Tim looked up to see Monica gathering Luke and Brian to her like a shepherdess. She looked beautiful standing by the entrance, a hand on the back of each boy, hugging them to her. She was talking to Frank and smiling. Tim caught her eye and watched the smile flicker and die and struggle to return. They nodded at each other, and Monica and the boys left the building.

CHAPTER 27

The next day, all the kids in town were getting ready for school, packing up lunches, and climbing on buses. Monica sighed a deep sigh when the boys climbed on bus four. She always swore to take this day off, each year, to just enjoy the quiet. She had never managed it, and she was her own boss. She did have a ritual, though. She went in late, with a fancy coffee from The Cup, and she sat in her beautiful office and made a list of all the beautiful things that had happened over the summer.

She was parking for The Cup before she remembered watching Max turn from Wolf to man. She laughed; it was almost more important to get properly caffeinated than it was that the universe had shifted. She walked in, curious to see if she would think anything different about Max, or Harriet, for that matter. Harriet was definitely part of it, but was she a shifter?

The place was bustling, the end of the before-work rush, and Max and Harriet were whirling around behind the counter, taking care of customers, chatting and making coffees. Well, Harriet was chatting, Max was just being quiet and smiley. Monica always liked having him serve her, because it took less time than a chat with Harriet. She was always in a rush, so she appreciated the quiet service.

She got up to the counter and it was Max serving her. He gave her a quick look and a quiet nod when she said her order; it was the same she'd done many times before. Monica marveled at the ordinariness of the experience. Her whole world had basically shifted sideways. She groaned at her own word-choice humor and smiled.

"Nice to see you smile, Monica. I know it's been a doozy of a weekend for you," Harriet called across the counter, smiling.

Monica smiled back before she thought about it. It had been a doozy. Frank. Shifters. Strange things in the woods. Bears. Tim. Sigh. She got her coffee and went to get her milk. On the side of the cup, Max had printed her name in black ink, "Mama Bear." Monica laughed out loud and looked over to see Max smirking into the next coffee he was making.

"Nice, Max. Nice," she called over her shoulder as she walked out. This was going to be okay, she thought. It really was. Max was Max. Harriet was whatever she was, and it really was going to be okay.

CHAPTER 28

Bill called Tim over to his desk. "Well, we've still got one Wolf unaccounted for. Max has been all over the woods in the past week, and he finds no further signs."

"How does he account for the Wolf presence here, Bill? And for the strangeness of their behavior?"

"He's really got no idea. When he left that old pack, he cut all his ties, so he doesn't have anyone to ask. Harriet knows some people up north, from her days as a traveler, so she's putting the word out, but we've got nothing but a bunch of strange Wolves up at the Council these days. They're not responding to treatment, so the healers are just leaving them be, keeping them comfortable. I haven't seen them, but Max says it's scary. They're almost like pets, is how he described it." It was possibly the worst thing a shifter could imagine, having the wildness of their animal side muted, or domesticated, in that way. The wildness brought with it an exhilarating freedom.

"Do we need to be worried about this lone Wolf?" Tim asked.

"Pfft," said Bill. "We do, yeah. As far as we know, he could be like the others, damaged, somehow. But we don't know that he is, and we don't know where he is, or what he wants. So, I'm going to keep patrols on the double until something happens." Tim nodded. "Hey, Tim, why didn't you tell us that Monica shafted you on the Mathewson thing? Alice told me about it. She was pissed. I mean, we need to play nice because she's on the Town Council, but she's not the only one on it. We can go around her just fine."

Tim thought for a minute. "No, it's all right, it was just a misunderstanding. Evidently, she's still getting over her ex, and the whole thing set her on fire in terms of PTSD-type stuff. It's not in her character, generally. I mean, the woman has a temper, but she's really committed to this town, just not to me." Tim sighed and wiped his hand across his face. "I don't expect anything like it to happen again. We certainly won't work together again. And we both know she's the best one on the whole Town Council."

Bill nodded. "Okay. I'll take your word for it. I'm sorry it didn't work out with you two. I thought she was a good match for you, in terms of strength, and clearly, your Bear thought so. You never did bite her, right? That can't be undone, you know. It's an old form of claiming a mate; it's been a long time since I've heard of anyone doing it instinctually. Some shifters do it in their wedding ceremony."

Tim just nodded. He'd been struck by the feeling several times but hadn't acted on it. Biting a woman wasn't really his style, shifter or not. And Monica *was* a good match for him, strong as she was. She could do anything, really. She was raising two good kids, singlehandedly. She was a businesswoman, who had made a career doing what she loved. A devoted sister. What else, exactly, did he want? She was undeniably sexy. It felt like ages since he'd been with her. Thinking of her writhing beneath him gave Tim a bit of a charge and he felt himself hardening up. He shook his head to clear his thoughts.

"I never acted on that particular impulse, thankfully. Okay, Bill, I'm going to get out of here. I've got to check in with Max and Harriet before heading out today. Billy needs a slew of things for school that I waited too long to get, and now, he's in school without all the extras he needs. The daycare already called me that he's not got his proper backup clothes, something about needing Fall now?" Tim sighed.

"Okay, Tim, See you soon. Billy's fine, remember? Extra wipes aren't what's important in his life. He's got you, and he's got us. Cut yourself some slack. You're doing a great job."

Tim smiled at his brother. "Thanks, Pops. Really, thanks, Bill."

Tim headed off, still smiling. Support from his family really did fill him with confidence. His chest swelled with love for all of them. His relationships with his brothers were complicated, but full of love and support. Another reason he totally got Monica. Her love for Frank was plainly obvious. Tim thought she worried too much, but Frank seemed to like it. He laughed to himself. Families were weird.

Tim drove around to The Cup and checked in with Max and Harriet. Everything seemed fine; it was a little slow as it was between rushes. Harriet greeted him with a boisterous, "Hey, Papa Bear!" and Max snorted. They seemed to exchange some kind of shared joy at this, and Tim just raised his eyebrows.

The two of them confirmed that everything was calm as far as the Wolves went. Max shook his head about the behavior of the Wolves they'd found. "It's entirely freaky, Tim. I've never seen or heard of anything like it. We've just got to wait and see, I think, as hard as that is."

Harriet agreed. "I've put out the call throughout the

shifter communities in this state, all of them. If we can gather information now, it might help us if more Wolves arrive. It's better to be prepared than caught off guard. It almost seems like an illness, but I know how insidious shifter attacks can be. If this is a form of attack, I'm completely at a loss."

Tim nodded.

Max spoke up. "Monica was just here. It's the first day of school for the boys and she always has a huge smile on. I remember it from last year. She almost glows. It's like the good in her finally pushes through her tough shell. She was heading over to her office."

Tim furrowed his eyebrows. Why was Max telling him this? "Okay, thanks, guys. I've got to get Billy's school stuff together. Typical dad, I waited till he was actually *in* school to start getting ready."

Harriet smiled. "You're doing a fantastic job, Tim. Billy is a great kid, and you are a great dad. Who cares about extra pencils? Billy will never care about extra pencils, Tim. He's got you."

Today was a good day, Tim thought, as he headed out to the mall. Friends and family were strong supports, and Billy *was* doing fine. Really, what more could he ask for? He headed into the stationary store to pick up the giant notebook he liked to get Billy for drawing in. *A fresh one for the new year*, he thought. Billy would be pleased.

He turned the corner into the aisle and was greeted by Monica's ass. She was bending over, trying to reach something at the back of a low-lying shelf. His Bear roared to life and he was immediately hard. His cheeks were flushed with embarrassment, and he tried to turn around and get out of that aisle without being seen.

But Monica had already noticed him. She had gotten down on her hands and knees, still rummaging at the back of the shelf. She turned her head and looked him over, completely oblivious to his hard-on.

"Tim? What are you doing here? I confess, the notebook aisle at the stationary store is one place I never thought I'd see you," she smiled.

Tim was ridiculously happy that she smiled at him. No venom and no awkwardness. She did seem to be glowing.

"I'm here to get Billy some of his new school year stuff. I like to get him a fresh drawing pad each fall, to mark the event. I'm a little late this year, but I don't think he'll notice." Tim chuckled. "What are you doing here? Don't you have a business to run?" he kidded.

Monica smiled again. She was so relaxed; it was almost miraculous. She plopped back to sit down on the floor of the aisle. "You're such a good dad, Tim. Really. Billy's lucky," she said. "I do sort of the same thing; the school year is a fresh start for me. I write a list of beautiful things that happened over the summer, and it starts my notebook for the year. So, I spend a little time picking out a nice one each year."

"That's a really nice tradition, Monica. Maybe I'll introduce it to Billy. Don't know if he can remember much of the summer, beyond the Bouncy Hut," he laughed.

Monica smiled ruefully. "These kids have no goddamned gratitude, Tim," she laughed. "Sorry for my language. I usually save it for family. You must've made the list when you fixed up Frank's place for him. I don't think I ever really thanked you for that. It really saved him. It means the whole world to me that he be happy and feel safe."

Tim crouched down next to her. "Mon, I would always help Frank out. He's my friend, and he's your brother. It matters to me. You matter to me. I'm really sorry for how everything played out. I definitely do want to be friends, if you are willing."

Monica could smell the warm tang of Tim's skin, clean

and crisp. *Oh my God*, she thought. *He smells so good. I don't want to be friends with this guy. I want him all over me, all the time. He was so good. Good.* It was now or never.

She cleared her throat, blinked twenty-eight times or so and took a giant and brave leap. "I don't want to be friends, Tim, I want more than that. Back like it was, but better, with all our cards on the table. I know you were really clear at bowling, but I don't think I can just be friends now. I feel more than that." Monica stood up, offered Tim her hand to pull him up. It was an awkward pull up, and Tim caught himself on Monica's hips. He did not let go.

"I'm... are you sure, Monica? I'm a mixed bag, you know. There's a whole lot you don't know."

"Well. I've just learned about Wolf shifters, Tim. I'm doing pretty well on that one, I think. Just tell me. Cards on the table. I can only deal with it if I know about it. Let me try, please? I can't guarantee what my face will do but just give me time, and I'll get there, I swear." Monica chuckled half-heartedly. "Please, Tim, just spill it."

Tim looked down at Monica's hips. He was still holding on for dear life. *This is one of those moments, those moments that change everything,* he thought. "Mon, I... I don't want you to run away from me because you don't understand. Just promise me you will stand still for 30 seconds at least, after I tell you. I mean it, you have to count and everything."

Monica snorted. "Tim, come on. It cannot be that bad." She held up her hand at Tim's look of concern. "Okay, ok, I promise. 30 seconds."

Tim tightened his hold on the fabric at her waist.

"Ok, Mon, here we go. Hold on to me, too. I need it." Monica grabbed his shoulders, looking around to be certain no one was watching the crazy couple in the journal section, holding on to each other like drowning people. "Mon. No matter what happens, you gotta know how much I want to be in your life, your kids' lives, all of it. I want to watch your face all day long, and all night." Tim broke off. He looked down at the ground. He felt like it was going to swallow him whole. *What if she ran away?*

"Tim, just say it. Get it out." Monica squeezed his shoulders.

"I'm a Bear Shifter, Mon." Tim whispered.

Monica's hands froze on his shoulders. Tim looked up to see her blinking rapidly. Her mouth was twitching, and her eyes were flashing more brilliantly than he'd ever seen. "Count." he said.

Monica's mouth made fish shapes as Tim held onto her waist, and out came the first "one". Tim whispered again, "Monnie, ask me questions. I know they're there."

"Are you safe? Is Billy a cub? Am I – wait, I've already seen your penis, can I have a bear baby? Would you eat me if you were a bear? Are my kids okay with you?"

Tim's eyes were wide, watching the torrent of questions fly from her mouth. He knew he had to give her time, knew he had to wait out this flood. Tim said, "Two, Three, Four." Monica took a deep breath and looked at Tim's face. He smiled at her, still holding on. Her hands moved again on his shoulders. "Ready? Keep going?" Tim asked.

Monica nodded. Now it was Tim's turn to take a deep breath. "Billy is not a cub. He will shift for the first time when he hits puberty. It is hard at first, but controlling it is a matter of practice. Billy will learn like I did, and all of my brothers, *all* of my brothers, Mon, and my father." Monica's eyes widened. "Five, Six, Seven, Eight, Nine." Tim counted softly. "Of course, I am safe, I am a lifelong protector of Mossy Ridge, from all the things that go bump in the night. And of course, your boys are safe with me. Safer than anywhere else, forever. Ten."

Monica looked down at the ground. Tim could see her

face shifting again but he didn't know what this one meant. "What, Mon? What is it? Ask me."

Monica looked up at him with tears in her eyes. "My kids are safe- with you, forever... I am safe with you? Keep counting, goddammit, keep counting." She closed her eyes tight. Tim didn't know if he should laugh or cry, but he was so relieved that she was swearing, he felt he might float off the ground.

"Eleven. Twelve. Thirteen. Fourteen. Fifteen.... More, Mon? You have more? We're halfway. Can I let you go? Are you going to run?"

Monica tightened her hands on his shoulders, bunching up the fabric in her fists. "I am not running, Tim. But you cannot let me go, okay? Sixteen. Seventeen. Eighteen. You cannot let me go, damnit. I'm in it, I don't know what it is, but I am all in with you, from here on in."

Tim had his eyes closed. He was caught in a maelstrom of emotion. He couldn't believe that she knew now. And she was still standing here and letting him touch her. His Bear wanted him to take her right now, wanted to bite and fuck and bite and fuck. He was flooded with pent-up animal desire, but wanted to do right by Monica, and treat her with the respect she deserved, not ravish her in the notebook aisle. He couldn't believe she knew about his being a shifter. It loosened an enormous reservoir of possibility and the flood was unstoppable.

"Tim?" she asked, "We're at Nineteen already. I don't understand. I mean, I really don't but I want you to tell me all the bits and pieces that I don't know, until it all makes sense, makes you." Monica took a deep breath. "Twenty."

Tim was slowly coming back to the surface, after fighting down his Bear. He opened his eyes and pulled her hips close to his. "Twenty-one. Monica, I am okay. I've actually never told anyone that I loved about being a shifter. Terri knew from the start and I never had to tell anyone or take the risk that they would reject me." He exhaled. "Twenty-two. I cannot tell you how much I love the way you are, the way you sift things down to what matters. I want you in all the ways, all the ways that there are. I'm completely in love with you."

Monica's face lit up. "You are in love with me?" Her eyes went wide, and she looked around the stationary aisle. She started to step back but Tim's hands kept her firmly anchored. "Twenty-three. Twenty-three. Twenty-three." Monica said quickly. "You are in love with me. Me? Have you met me? I mean, I am a piece of work, Tim."

Tim laughed out loud. "That's three twenty-threes Mon, I think that puts us at twenty-five. Twenty-six. I am in love with *you*. And also, I'm a little bit complicated too, Mon. I mean, I am a *bear shifter*. Did I mention that one?"

Monica laughed. "Oh My God. You win." There was a pause. "You really love me Tim? Are you sure?" She looked up at him. Tim moved her body closer to his.

"I've never been more certain of anything in my life, Monnie. Twenty-seven."

Monica tucked her head down into Tim's chest and breathed in his scent. "I think you can be done with counting, Tim. I'm not going anywhere." She looked up at him and winked, "unless you say sixty-nine."

Tim laughed out loud. "Monica... I swear to god, I'm going to order you pizza and feed you beer and give you lots and lots of good sex. We're fulfilling dreams starting now. No kids are anywhere nearby for the next four hours. If you'll let me, I'd love to take you someplace with a real bed. It should be enough time, but barely. I definitely can't guarantee you any sleep."

Monica reached around and cupped Tim's ass. "I don't

know, Tim. What's it going to be like in a bed? With all that space? You could lose me."

Tim growled. "I will not lose you ever again. I love you in all the ways, Mon. All the ways."

Monica felt her skin flush. This was the real deal and they both knew it. She led the way out of the store, and they each drove to Monica's house. The time separated in the cars was enough time to clarify things for Monica. She definitely wanted this; it wasn't some flash of hormone, or loneliness. This was Tim, and she was going to try her damnedest to make something real and certain and forever with him. She couldn't think of a man she respected more.

It was happening the same way for Tim, in his truck. He was so certain. He knew they were both flawed, and had their pasts still to deal with fully, but he was certain that Monica was the one for him. His Bear growled happily.

The two cars pulled into Monica's driveway, and Tim and Monica got out at the same time. It felt marital, almost, the approach to the house. This was the first time of many first times for them. It really struck them both, and they headed in, holding hands, quietly, but smiling.

*S*ix months later

THERE WAS LITTLE QUIET IN THEIR LIVES. THREE BOYS, NOISE, crashes, and an expectation of profanity at any minute, was par for the course. Most of the profanity came from Monica, but not all, to her chagrin. Her quirk had spread, and Tim was not innocent. The new family had a hard and fast rule that it was just family, though, and the boys were all well-mannered and polite in the outside world.

The Mathewson Project was moving forward, many of the houses were already built and just awaiting final approval to be inhabited. Monica was very proud and excited to see the work completed. More than one family had asked for the homes to be furnished, so her design company was happily benefiting as well, all above board.

Tim and Bill were still calling for double patrols, but nothing had happened. Max had his suspicions, but it seemed that Mossy Ridge was in a comfortable limbo, and most were content with that. Harriet still had her fingers in some pies throughout the state and would be the first to know if things changed anywhere.

Monica usually loved the summer best; she had the boys fulltime, and the weather was divine. But, this year, sharing the winter with a full house of boys had proven to be spectacular. It was sometimes overwhelming, the noise and smells, but Tim was an involved, equal partner, and it made for much more fun than work. She was wildly in love with him and it was clear to all who saw them. Tim was equally in love and, often, the sight of the two of them in town brought smiles to the faces of strangers who knew that kind of love.

They met on a school day at The Cup, after splitting to deliver the boys to their busses or daycare. Max gave them a nod and walked away without taking their order. It was the same all the time, so he just went and put their coffees together.

Tim smiled. He'd never expected to feel so grounded in his life, and so clear that he was exactly where he was supposed to be. Monica raised her eyebrows and whispered to Tim, "What if I want to change my fucking order? What then?"

Tim laughed out loud. "Monica. In six months, you've ordered exactly the same thing every time I've been with you. You want something else? We'll just order it. Don't blame Max for knowing your tastes."

It was Monica's blush that did him in today. She blushed and sighed. "I guess I want to be less goddamned predictable. Am I boring?"

Tim looked at her seriously. "I have a very good idea of where we can find out how boring you are, Mons, but it means going back home, right now. You can show me how unpredictable you can be."

Monica stood a little taller. "Actually, Tim, I think that is an amazing idea." She rolled her shoulders back, "I've been thinking about one thing, in particular, and it has to do with those kitchen counters you cleaned yesterday. You game?"

Tim coughed. "Yes ma'am, I think I am."

With that, they sent some texts, and headed home.

* * *

Thanks so much for reading Enemy Daddy Bear! I hope you loved it! If you did then I'm pretty sure you will love another series we have, this one called the Bridge Hollow Shifters, from Samantha Leal…

Click here to read the Bridge Hollow Shifters Complete Collection, here on Amazon.

TROUBLE IS COMING TO BRIDGE HOLLOW - A STRANGE mountain town full of mystery...where nothing is as it seems…

WITH A SIX WEEK BREAK TO FILL AND PLENTY TO RUN FROM, timid teacher Amanda decides it's time to break the mold and go on a random road trip with her best friend to the mysterious town of Bridge Hollow.

BRIDGE HOLLOW IS FAMOUS FOR ITS STRANGE HAPPENINGS AND shifter legends, but skeptic Amanda just wants to chill out for the summer and catch her breath after a particularly rough breakup.

But of course anything she gets involved in is bound to be "complicated", and this town – and town alpha Dean - are no exception. From a wildlife die off to the volatile locals tempers flaring at the slightest provocation – there is definitely something strange going on in this paranormal tourist trap.

As Dean pulls his pack together to avert a firestorm, will Amanda be his 'ace in the hole' or a weakness he can't afford?

Here is a brief preview of Alpha Daddy Bear, the first story in the Bridge Hollow series…

Bridge Hollow – Present Day

THE WOODS WERE DARK AS THE TWO MEN MADE THEIR WAY across the bubbling stream. The rocks were slippery under-foot, the water flowing fast, and they steadied themselves against each other as to not to lose their footing.

"It's cold out here," David said as he stopped and exhaled. He couldn't fully tell with there being so little light, but he thought he may have seen a wisp of icy air clinging to his breath as he spoke, and it sent a chill right down his spine.

"I've never seen it like this," his companion, Ben, said as he stopped and hitched his gun up onto his broad shoulder. "Maybe that's why we're not getting much luck…" he clicked his teeth and sighed as he looked back down the stream, towards the folds of trees that were bending and dipping across them from overhead. The branches were thick and full of green, but even with that considered, these two hunters were used to this forest. They knew it like the back of their hands, and both could tell that there was something strange happening there around them.

This day, something was very, very different indeed.

"It's the middle of summer," David said. "This place should be crawling with deer."

Ben shrugged and reached into his back pocket for a pack of smokes. He clamped one between his teeth and reached for a lighter.

"Oh, that's a great idea," David snorted with a wry smile. "That'll really attract the animals."

Ben rolled his eyes and lit up anyway. He sucked in deeply and exhaled before he turned and climbed up and over the rocks, onto the muddy side of the embankment and out of the chill of the water.

"Thing's ain't been right round here for a while,' he said as he crouched down and ran his fingertips into the ground. The earth was threateningly cold, with a force he had never known before. It wasn't just the cool soil in the shadows, this was something deep from within. Something menacing and raw.

"This fucking town," he whispered. "If it's not crazed tourists flooding the streets looking for Bigfoot or whatever the hell they believe, it's the locals slowly going insane with the rumors and legends."

"Well maybe it's high time we stopped coming here then," David said goadingly. "But I think we all know what brings you to these parts. You can mock the tourists all you want, but what you're looking for is your own juicy piece of the pie."

The men looked at each other knowingly and Ben took one last drag before he stubbed out his cigarette on the base of his boot, threw the butt into the gush and pull of the stream and started to laugh.

"May as well," he winked as he let his rifle drop to the floor beside his feet and then he sat with his legs dangling over the ridge.

David climbed up beside him and the pair sat together looking around. For a summer's day the forest was bleak and freezing. It was not long past noon, and they were right to be wary. It was clear to them both, as seasoned hunters, that something was amiss out there.

"Do you think it's Bigfoot coming to get us?" David joked as he reached for his water bottle and took a long, deep sip.

"Don't be foolish," Ben replied. "It is something though, alright."

The sun was nowhere to be seen, but there didn't appear

to be a cloud in the sky. The break in the trees above showed blue, but there was something strange about it. Something other-worldly. The air was still and chilly, like a veil had descended and trapped them there in their own little bubble.

"Come on," David got to his feet and stretched before he reached down and scooped up his rifle and slung it back over his shoulder. "We may as well get out of here. It's a lost cause. If we go fast we'll get the best part of the afternoon over in the bar instead, the wives don't need to know a thing."

Ben laughed and nodded. David helped him up and they began to walk further into the forest.

The men crunched over the earth and when Ben looked down he was sure he saw a frost forming. As they got further into the trees and closer to the center which would allow them to cross back over to where they had parked on the outskirts, the woods got darker still and the air became prickly and vengeful.

Ben looked towards David and he could see his face darkening too. Neither of them spoke a word, but with each step forward they took, they were getting further and further away from the light, and further from the world they knew. They were descending into something unknown. Something dark and powerful. As they stepped through a thick section of trees and emerged into a clearing, Ben's breath caught in his throat and his whole body was shocked with cold. It pierced him deep within his heart and kept him there, paralysed with fear.

David stopped too, and Ben was aware of the rifle falling again. Down to the ground, crunching onto the frost under their feet and turning icy and white as it connected with the earth.

"My God," Ben gasped. His eyes widened as he took in the scene in front of him.

For a moment, he was sure that he must be dreaming.

None of this could be real. He blinked and lifted his shaking hands towards his eyes where he tried to rub them, but the cold wouldn't allow his fingers to move. They were frozen in place, quickly turning red and frost bite taking hold.

"Dav…id…" his voice cracked. The cold travelled through his mouth and right down to the pit of his stomach. It gripped him like nothing he had ever known before and within a second it was as if he were turning to stone.

Before them both, as they stood there freezing, the last things their eyes saw was the scene in the forest.

The trees above them were turned brown and black, their trunks and roots poisoned from the ground up. A fog was heavy in the air, something dank and sweet, trails of energy wisping up from the cracks in the earth below. The circle in the center of the clearing. The darkness and the death. Heaps and heaps of bodies. Animals of the woods that had gathered there, in that very spot and met their end, just like Ben and David themselves. The circle of bears, wolves, deer, rabbits, racoons and birds were all piled together, in a swirling pattern, all facing the central point of the clearing.

It was like something out of a horror movie. Something unnatural, dark and magical. But not the good kind of magical. Something utterly terrifying. Whatever had come to the woods of Bridge Hollow had managed to kill off at least a hundred animals. Either they had been led to their death, or they had been called.

Now Ben and David were a part of them. They would never make it to the bar on Main Street, and they would never get to tell their wives what they had seen that day. They would certainly never hunt again.

Some would have said that was a good thing.

Some would think it terrible luck.

But for the animals of Bridge Hollow, it was only just the beginning. They may not have had Bigfoot lurking around them, but they sure as hell had something. And now it was coming out to play in full force.

The cold slowly began to lift, and the animals sank into the ground like it was quicksand, taking David and Ben along with them. Like the saying often went, the ground opened and swallowed them whole. Slowly and silently, one by one. Any evidence of what had occurred there was completely destroyed, taken away as if it had never happened at all.

The darkness lifted, but the chill remained.

The sun broke through the trees and lit up the clearing, the fog cleared, but the energy there would be forever changed. There was something magical about this place. Something deep and meaningful. Something that the locals were either going to have to embrace or fight.

Bridge Hollow was never going to be the same again...

You know you want to visit Bridge Hollow... a new town
with new mysteries ...
...Get it here on Amazon ...;)

www.ingramcontent.com/pod-product-compliance
Lightning Source LLC
Chambersburg PA
CBHW071623150726
48000CB00004B/1861